DEMIGODS ACADEMY

HOURS OF OLYMPUS

BOOK 8

D1598845

DEMIGODS ACADEMY

HOURS OF OLYMPUS

ELISA S. AMORE

KIERA LEGEND

CHAPTER ONE

NICOLE

$\mathcal{T}$he sandy ground shook beneath us as Cade, Tinker, and I, hid crouched behind the large, jagged outcropping of rocks at the edge of the beach. Out of the corner of my eye, I saw a huge, black, fire-breathing horse thunder out of the tall and spiky reeds lining the seaside—its muscles rippling in the light.

A man clad from head-to-toe in shiny armor rode on the beast's back—at least I thought it was a man, it was hard to tell from this angle. The armor glinted as he unsheathed his massive broad sword, and with a ululating war cry that made me shake in fear, he charged into the fray. I didn't know exactly who he was, but I knew he was one of the Gods, and he was terrifying.

I stuck my head around the rocks to risk a peek at what was happening. I mean, a war was going on—that much was obvious by the gathering of troops and the clanging of metal swords and shields. There was also the roar of three headed giants as they waved their hundred muscular arms around, trying to hit something, anything.

The earth quivered beneath them, and beneath the flappling of massive blue wings from the huge dragon above us. Its ice breath shot mercilessly from its mouth, leaving a trail of frigid spikes in its wake.

It was a war between the Gods and Titans, after all. One for the history books. Literally.

A war that had occurred over three thousand years ago. Cade, Tinker, and I, just happened to time travel here by the unexpected turn of a tiny knob on my simple pocket watch, something I still didn't even remember. Well, obviously not so simple after all.

It was a shocking surprise to me, and to Cade, since he was the one who crafted it for me as a gift, way back when we were friends. Before I did something horrible, got expelled from the academy, and had all my memories erased as punishment.

It still seemed like a dream.

"Don't! You'll get killed." Cade grabbed the back of my shirt and tried to pull me back to his side, the fabric stretching tightly against my torso as he did.

I jerked out of his grip. "I'm not going to die from looking."

Tinker made a few scared peeps and bloops. The little robot was obviously in agreement with Cade. He was actually quivering inside his small, round body, but that didn't stop me; I had to see what was happening. Me and curiosity were BFFs, even when indulging it wasn't the best idea. Sure, that friendship had gotten me into all kinds of dangerous and precarious situations, but I lived for that shit. Life was way too boring without it.

My gaze returned to the fight just in time to see the intimidating Goddess Athena fly into the fray. I recognized her from seeing her at the academy—her molded chest plate, arm, and wrist cuffs glinting under the hot sun. She landed at a run on the sand, and unsheathed her huge sword as she moved, pointing it at the sky.

Above her, the sun seemed to draw closer, which was obviously impossible. Still, it looked like its pale rays grew stronger, their heat intensifying until it felt like prickles on my skin. A huge man in gold armor swooped down from beyond the wispy clouds, landing just on the edge of the crashing white surf.

It was so bright that I had to squint to see him. Between the gaps in his helmet, light and fire flared from inside.

"Hyperion!" Athena shouted. "I've been waiting for you!"

"Here I am." His fire erupted from inside his helmet and suit of armor, and blinding light flashed all around him. It was like a nuclear bomb had been released, radiating pure power, and I wasn't quick enough to close my eyes or shield them with my hand.

"Shit!" I pulled back, rapidly blinking, but I couldn't force away the sunspots in my vision. I winced; the dancing white flecks were nearly painful in their intensity.

Cade's hand gripped my shoulder with concern, but the feeling was reassuring. "What happened?"

"Some dude made of fire just blinded me." I rubbed at my eyes, but it wasn't helping. In fact, it appeared to be making it worse. It felt like I was rubbing sand into my skin. I'd once heard that the whites of your eyes didn't have any nerve endings, and so, you couldn't feel pain there, but right at that moment I begged to differ.

"I told you not to look."

"Well, technically, you said, *"Don't, you'll get killed."*"

"We need to get off this beach and to a safe place."

I turned my head toward him, but could only see a vague outline of his body as it moved. It was incredibly disorienting.

"Tink, you need to change your wheels to tracks, because we're going to need to go fast, and I can't carry you and Nicole out of here."

"I don't need to be carried." I huffed, raising my chin into the air.

"Can you see this?"

I felt, rather than saw, what I was sure was his hand waving in front of my face, and squinted at the blurry dark form. Only instinct—and impossible familiarity—told me it was him, and not any old passerby. "Yes?"

"Oh, for fire and brimstone's sake! Could you please shut up?! You are distracting me."

My head lifted toward Hades's voice, but all I could grasp was a swirling mass of darkness on top of the sharp rocks. I'd almost forgotten he was there, what with being blinded and all. Honestly, he hadn't done much since we arrived, but stand there, look cool, and shout at his brothers now and then to *'smite that guy'* and another.

Based on all the hype about how dangerous the

Dark God was, I was a bit underwhelmed by him and his actions.

"Maybe a little help here, then?" Scowling at the lord of the underworld was probably not the best idea I'd ever had, but I couldn't help myself.

Cade huffed derisively. "You're wasting your time asking Hades for help. He's the most selfish God there is."

The mass of darkness jumped down from the rock to land right in front of us. Startled, Cade jumped beside me, before steeling himself.

"Am I, now? Interesting, as I do not even know you, boy."

"Nor will you," Cade snorted. "You'll be too busy idling your time away in the underworld to ever help with the academy—" he cursed under his breath, muttering something about time paradoxes and that he shouldn't spout things that hadn't happened yet.

"The underworld?" Hades loomed over us. "Tell me more."

The clang of steel echoed all around as the fighting beyond the rocks got louder.

"Aren't you going to do something?" I gestured toward the mayhem raging on the other side.

"About what?"

"About the war happening nearby?" I rapidly blinked at him, my eyesight starting to clear.

Hades brought his hands together, well, almost together, there was a few inches gap between them as he swirled them. Between his palms, a sphere of darkness formed. It was so black, I sensed that if I touched it, I'd lose my finger inside it. Like it would literally vanish inside the void he'd just created.

Once a ball the size of a basketball formed, Hades drew his arm back and fired it over the rocks. I wasn't entirely sure what happened, or who it hit, but a pain-laced scream pierced through the cacophony of noise.

"Satisfied?" he questioned.

Cade grabbed my hand. "Get ready. I'm flying us out of here."

My attention turned to Hades. "Tell your brother I said he's a wanker."

"Which brother? They are both quite bothersome."

"Zeus," I clarified. "Tell him he can shove that thunder bolt of his up his arse for what he does to me in the future."

Hades's bark of laughter was unexpected. "You are quite amusing. I have not laughed in years. Not since Hephaistos gave Ares boils all over his genitals for sleeping with his wife. *Again*." He slapped the top of my head and instantly my eyesight cleared.

I could see again, but now I had a headache, because he hadn't been gentle.

"Now, go. Before I get bored and decide to turn both of you into goats, then feed you to the cyclopes as reward for siding with the Gods during this tedious war."

His hands moved in front of him again, but this time, a wall of shadow formed near us. "It will hide you from the enemy as you flee."

"Thanks, mate," I barely got the words out before Cade yanked me to him, wrapped an arm around my waist, and took us into the air.

As we flew, not too fast or Tinker wouldn't be able to keep up on the ground, I turned my head back to the beach and the battle raging there. Cade had said it was going to be a blood bath, and he wasn't wrong.

Limbs from giants and humanoid beasts, as well as tentacles from squid-like monsters littered the shore. The sand was no longer beige, but pink, and in some spots, crimson red. Waves crashed onto the beach, trying desperately to wash away the carnage but failed. There was just too much of it.

"We'll find a safe spot near those cliffs and figure out what Tinker did to the watch so we can get back to the academy."

"What if we can't figure it out?" My stomach

churned at the thought, but we had to consider the possibility. Not doing it would've been stupid.

Cade's face paled. "Let's just get to safety first."

He swooped down, taking us toward a craggy rock formation. Some fruit trees and a stream stretched below in the valley. As we got closer though, I had to shake my head because I swore the mountain was moving.

A thunderous crack and groan reverberated in the wind, until the stone seemed to unfold itself. Then the rocks slowly turned, crackling as they went, and a pair of large brown eyes made of mossy boulders with tree branches for eyelashes, blinked down at us.

"Holy shit!" I cried out, just as the mountain started to walk, nearly hitting us with its solid gray mass of a shoulder.

Cade veered sharply to the right, nearly making me slip out of his arms. I doubled my efforts of holding onto him, by wrapping my hands in the fabric of his shirt—I didn't want to fall again. That had sucked the first time it happened, and I didn't need that kind of stress right now.

Dumbfounded, we watched as the rocky and wooden giantess strode toward the beach. She was obviously joining the battle. I felt bad for the Gods who had to fight her.

Despite there being an entire piece of the terrain missing, Cade flew us down to the stream. It was still a good spot to reconvene, even without the protection from the sun, wind, and rain that a mountain provided.

The second my feet touched ground, I sank to the soft grass gracefully, before I fell like a lump of silly putty. My knees were having a hard time staying solid.

"Who the hell was that rock giantess, do you know?"

Cade's hands scrubbed his face, and I could tell that he was having a hard time keeping it together, but I appreciated that he was making an effort.

"From what I know about the Titans, I'd say that was Mnemosyne, the Goddess of Memory and Time."

"Time? Maybe she can help us get back."

He threw me a dubious look. "Do you want to be the one to go ask her for help? Not sure she'd have time between stomping on Gods and tearing others limb by limb."

"Yeah, okay. Point taken." Stretching my legs in front of me, I felt relieved for the slight reprieve from the chaos we'd transported into today. The babbling of the stream was almost enough to drown out the sounds of fighting in the distance. It was a pretty spot, considering the hell being unleashed just through the woods and over the rise.

Cade crouched near the stream, cupped some water and brought it to his mouth to drink. Watching him made me realize just how dry my throat was. I was about to crawl over to his side, when he came over, carrying a cup made of leaves with water inside. He handed it to me, and I drank it greedily.

After I was done, I inspected the leaf cup he'd fashioned. "Impressive. I thought you didn't have earth powers."

"No, I said they weren't as good as my other ones."

"Then I'm doubly impressed." I shrugged. "A boast without being an ego maniac."

Sitting down beside me on the grass, he chuckled and took out the watch from his pocket, turning it around in his fingers. "Now, to figure out what Tinker did to the watch."

As if conjured by simply speaking his name, Tinker came shooting out of the woods, his little tracks whirring loudly from the effort of going off-roading. Squinting at him while he wheeled closer, I realized he carried something in his little metal arms. It was wrapped in a white cloth, and it squirmed in his hold.

"Nicole, Cade, look what I found in the woods!"

My heart dropped into my stomach when I realized he was carrying a baby.

CHAPTER TWO

NICOLE

Stunned, I looked down at the burbling, squirming, tiny infant who was swaddled in a white cloth, and cuddled in Tinker's thin metal arms. My first thought was that it couldn't possibly be real, but a second glance told me that it had to be. It had wide, shining eyes that wheeled frantically from one of us to the next, flailing fists, and skin that looked pink and soft.

Yeah. Not that I had a lot of experience with kids or anything, but I was pretty sure that was a real baby.

"How in the hell did you find a baby, Tinker?" Cade studied the infant over my shoulder, his expression wary. It was funny that he didn't want to get closer to it, like it was a bomb or something—just as sinister and deadly. In fact, he looked a bit like he'd encountered a wild mythical creature, rather than a small, squiggling human.

"As I rolled through the trees, I heard a tiny cry. I followed the sound and found the baby in a bed of moss. It smiled at me."

I looked into Tinker's eyes and thought that if he could cry, there'd be drops of oil coming out right about now. My own eyes prickled, and I blinked rapidly to try to hold wetness back.

But... the poor little thing.

"I had to pick it up and take it with me. I couldn't leave it all alone to die."

"Are you sure its parents weren't nearby?" I asked, looking around uneasily; worried that someone was going to point at us and yell *baby snatchers!* "Maybe they set the baby down to go get some food or something."

That wouldn't be a stellar parenting choice by any means, but it was possible.

Glancing at the infant for a long moment, he made a low bloop, the sound somehow containing a wealth of emotion. I had a sense that maybe he hadn't considered that, maybe he'd been too excited about finding a baby, and it was now just dawning on him. "Oh."

Cade shook his head, still eyeing it like it was seconds away from growing a second head. "The last thing we need is to take care of some baby. We can't take it with us."

"Well, we can't leave it here," I argued. "That would be horrible and cruel, Cade. I never pictured you acting like a villain." My fingers pulled back the cloth protecting the infant's face. Its eyes widened, and a tiny hand reached up and wrapped around my finger. Despite my best efforts, I felt my heart thud. *Shit. That's not fair, little baby.*

"I'm not trying to be horrible and cruel, but we have other matters that we need to deal with. Like how the hell we get home and back to our time period?"

"I totally get that, but at least we could look for a village nearby. There has to be mortals around. Obviously." I gestured to the baby. "We can find some couple to give the baby to."

"What if it's not a mortal baby?" Cade asked.

I frowned. "What do you mean?"

"There are tons of stories about Gods having relations with mortals and begetting other Gods and Demigods."

My frown deepened as I studied the baby, looking for any type of characteristic that would identify it as inhuman. Horns maybe, a tail. Pink eyes or something.

"Who do you think this is, then? Because we can't exactly go back to the beach, wave it around and ask, 'Hey, whose baby is this?'"

He shrugged, making no effort to get any closer. "I don't know. Could be any number of them. Heracles maybe. Or Perseus."

Gently, I held out my arms and took the baby from Tinker. It squirmed a little but didn't cry or fuss—even though my movements were awkward, because I had no idea how to hold an infant. At least, not that I remembered.

"It doesn't look muscle bound." I brought it over to Cade. It was comical the way he shrunk back from it, like it was somehow going to harm him, so I shook my head at him. "It's a baby not an explosive device."

"I know." Yet, he didn't look convinced.

His expression made me laugh again. "I can't believe we're in the middle of the Gods' war and you're afraid of a teeny tiny infant." I couldn't refrain from rolling my eyes.

Insulted, Cade huffed. Apparently, I'd hit a nerve. "I'm not afraid. I just don't want to hold it. How is that so easy for you?"

"I don't know." I shrugged. "Maybe I dealt with them before in my life, though I can't remember. Did I ever mention having a baby sister?"

Sadness entered his eyes as he shook his head. Actually, thinking about it made me sad too.

"Besides, we have other things to be concerned about."

"Okay, you're right. What do you suggest we do? What's our first course of action?"

"Find a village, I guess," he agreed. "There must be one around here. We can drop off the baby, get some food and water, and find a safe place to hunker down while we figure out the watch."

"Since you're the one with the wings, I guess you're on recon duty. Tinker and I will stay here and babysit."

Cade's wings unfurled, and he lifted into the air. I watched him rise, knowing I would never not think it was super cool, and that he was super hot when he flew. The golden boy, Lucian was like some huge golden eagle that was all show and flash, but Cade was like a falcon in the sky. Smaller, sleeker, faster, and, I couldn't deny it, *sexy*.

While he was gone, I took the baby to the stream, dipped my finger into the water and put it in its mouth. It sucked on my finger greedily, so I dipped it in water again. Unfortunately, I didn't have a bottle, or milk, so this would have to do until we could find someone to take care of it.

I kind of felt bad for thinking about the baby as an

"it", but I had no desire to unwrap the cloth and find out its gender. It was a bit rude, to be honest, and it didn't really matter anyway. However, I decided it needed a name.

"What's a good name for a baby, Tinker?"

A couple of thinking beeps echoed around us, and his head turned slightly as he glanced at me. "Baby?"

I smirked, shaking my head. "You have to think outside the box, Tink. You're thinking too literally." My eyes narrowed as I looked at our surroundings. I focused on some of the trees nearby. "How about we call the baby *Figgy?*" Because you found it among the fig trees."

A happy bleep escaped Tinker, and he rolled back and forth—his version of a happy dance, I guessed. "I like that name."

"Me too." Playfully tapping the baby's nose with my finger, I saw it gurgle at me. "Hello, Figgy."

No more than ten minutes later, Cade landed where we had huddled along the stream. "I spotted a few huts downstream. It looks like a small village. I didn't see any people, but I didn't go low enough."

"How far, do you think?"

"Not too far. An hour walk, maybe."

"Okay, let's drink some water, gather some food, then get going." I handed the baby back to Tinker, who immediately cradled it with expertise. "You can carry Figgy."

Cade's eyebrows arched dubiously. "You named the baby Figgy?"

A smile curved my lips. "Yeah. It's cute, right?"

He just shook his head and crouched next to the river, cupping some water and drinking.

After eating a few figs and gathering more to put in our pockets, we set out to walk along the riverbend to find the huts Cade had seen. Hopefully, we'd find some decent people to give Figgy to before we finally zapped ourselves out of here.

As we walked farther away from the beach, we could almost pretend there wasn't a war going on… if we also pretended not to see the flashes of lightning in the sky, or hear the shrieks of flying beasts overhead. Every time it happened, Tinker would juggle the baby with one arm while pointing with the other.

"Look!"

"Yeah, Tinker, I saw it. Just like the last ten times you pointed."

Cade was quiet during the trip. His attention remained on my pocket watch, which he held in his hand and kept looking at every few minutes.

I hoped he would come up with a solution, because honestly, I had no idea what had happened, or how to make it happen again. Also, I wasn't so sure that Tinker knew either. The little robot was probably just playing around with it, without any goal in mind, and accidentally triggered a time travel portal.

The farther along the stream we got, evidence of human existence started to emerge. Several worn paths were visible, leading from the woods to the river. It was possible they were made by animals, like deer, but the paths were a little wider, made by two people walking side by side perhaps? Then I spotted a large clay jug laying on its side on the shore across from us. Forgotten there, possibly? Or left there on purpose?

"We must be close." I pointed to it, noticing Cade's quick nod.

"Let's walk through the woods now, since the stream is veering away from where I spotted the huts." He unfurled his wings, probably with the intention of picking me up and flying me over the water, but I was tired of feeling useless and having to rely on him.

Backing up a few steps, I ran toward the river, leaping off the edge—my arms pinwheeling as I soared through the air. For a split second, I didn't think I'd jumped high enough and would land in the water, but then I hit the shore with the toe of my runner and propelled myself forward. My hands and knees hit the harsh ground when I landed on the rocks and shrubs.

Laughing, I got to my feet. A couple of scrapes appeared on my hands, but nothing bothersome, so I turned toward Cade on the other side.

"I could've just flown you there," he called.

"Yeah, but where's the fun in that?"

With a small sigh, he picked up Tinker, who clutched the baby close to his metal chest, and carried them over the water. He set them down as gently as he could next to me—considering the bulkiness of Tinker and heaviness I imagined the baby added.

Through it all, Figgy didn't even make a peep, though. Cade was probably right about the baby not being human.

The path that led into the trees became visible quickly. Cade went in first, but I made Tinker go next, even though he tried to argue with me about it. Once I said it was important to protect the baby, he relented, and I walked along the path last.

When we found someone to take the baby, I was sure Tinker would have a hard time letting go. Who knew the little robot would have such fierce parenting instincts? There was no way I would've programmed them into him. Another thought came to me, and I narrowed my eyes at Cade. I didn't think he would have programmed it either, so maybe Tinker had actually developed the emotions all on his own.

About halfway into the wooded glen, I got the sense that we were being watched. I scanned the foliage, spotting a few birds staring down at us from high branches. A small brown rabbit hopped across the path in front of me, but it wasn't their presence that was unnerving me.

Someone was in these woods with us right now, tracking our movements, like a predator monitoring its prey.

"Cade—" that was all the warning I managed to let out before we were surrounded by three young women.

Brown dyed togas covered their bodies while various animal pelts sat on their shoulders, like capes. All three carried sharpened spears, and they were pointed in our direction.

My hands instantly ignited in flames. The woman nearest to me startled a little, her eyes widened at the fire blooming in my hands, but she didn't lower her spear. With a Gods' war nearby, I suspected she was used to those with strange powers.

"Don't, Nicole," Cade cautioned and splayed his hands out to his sides—a defensive move to be sure. "We don't want to start a forest fire."

"I don't want to be skewered to death, either."

A few concerned bleeps and bloops escaped from Tinker, then he rolled out from between the two of us and raised his arms, presenting the baby to the women. He did it, I imagined, in hopes to diffuse the situation, or to call on the women's natural empathy.

What did happen surprised the shit out of me.

All three women lowered their spears, dropping to a single knee before the baby and bowing their heads.

So it was confirmed. Figgy was most definitely not human.

CHAPTER THREE

NICOLE

*T*he three women remained crouched for a long moment, solemn and respectful.

After they finally got back to their feet, they led us, with the gentle prodding of their spears, deeper into the woods and toward their small village. Although, even the "gentle prodding" with a sharp object still stung.

Once we arrived, we were immediately surrounded by at least thirty women—young and old—and several small satyrs, which were half man-half goat people. Everyone wanted to see the baby, but Tinker had Figgy pressed tightly to his metal chest, protecting the infant.

I could already tell that it was going to be difficult to get the little robot to give up the baby, despite it being the proper thing to do. Also, the way Figgy looked up at Tinker, happy and cooing, delighted by the way the dappled sunlight of the woods glinted on his metal frame, made it seem like the instant affection was mutual.

A tall, definitely over six feet, red-headed woman with piercing blue eyes, and the same sharp and angular face as the others, walked out of the biggest hut. She wore a crown of ivy on top of her head while all the others bowed their heads toward her. Her bearing was regal, nearly fierce.

Obviously, that was the person in charge, and I could definitely see why. She had a commanding way about her. She also looked like she could kick some serious ass. I'd kill for biceps like hers.

"Welcome, travelers," she called to us, narrowing her eyes in assessment. Her tone and gaze weren't exactly unfriendly, but I wouldn't call them warm and fuzzy either. "I am Lena. Priestess of this village."

Cade cleared his throat. "I'm Cade. This is Nicole…"

"I am Tinker." My robot beeped, and Figgy gurgled.

Lena's gaze settled onto Figgy, who squirmed a little

in Tinker's grip. "I have had many visions of you, Cade and Nicole. I witnessed your arrival. I saw that you would bring us *him*..." She gestured to the baby with reverence.

Unaware, Figgy drooled.

All the others dropped to a knee and bowed to him.

Tinker shied away from her though, pulling the baby in as close as he could. At his reaction, Lena's brow furrowed, and I wondered if she was going to do something to gain control over the small infant. We didn't need a complication like angering this woman right now.

Turning to Tinker, I reached for the infant. "Give me Figgy."

For a moment, I thought Tinker wasn't going to give up the baby, certain I had read frustration on his little robot face. However, he let out a long metallic sigh, and drew out his arms toward me. I took the burbling bundle from him gently, and faced Lena, bouncing the baby in my arms, which he seemed to like.

"Tinker found him in the woods. He was all alone."

Lena reached for Figgy, and I gave him to her, instantly missing the warmth of its soft pink skin. Lowering her head, the priestess pressed her lips to

Figgy's forehead and then lifted him in the air before the others. "Finally, we have our prince!"

Loud cheer erupted from the villagers, and they pumped their fists in the air.

Stepping closer to Cade, I leaned into him. "Now, do you know who Figgy is?"

"Let us feast!" Lena announced, victorious.

Before Cade could answer me, he was pulled away by one of the villagers just as I was taken by another, their firm grips not allowing me to resist.

"We must prepare for the festivities," the woman insisted and led me to one of the huts, ushering me inside of it with strong hands.

Nervous sounds fluttered off Tinker while he rolled in behind me, so I patted his dome head. "It's going to be fine. Nothing to be worried about." I eyed my companion. "Right?"

"Of course not." She gave me a sweet smile. "I am to help you bathe and get proper clothing on for the feast."

My attention dropped to my T-shirt and jeans, both smudged with dirt and dusted with beach sand. I was pretty sure I could feel the tiny granules in my hair, abrading my scalp so I could indeed do with a change of clothes.

"The clothes I will happily take, but I'm sure I can bathe myself, thank you."

After arguing with her for a good ten minutes, I was able to take off my clothes behind a privacy screen, and sink into a wooden tub full of hot water—made fragrant with petals from various flowers. The girl, whose name was Agatha, also gave me a cloth to clean myself.

Instead of fighting it, which I soon realized was basically pointless since we were stuck there for a while anyway, I indulged myself for a few minutes and closed my eyes, letting the steamy bath ease the stiffness in my muscles and bones. I hadn't had a moment to myself in days to chill out and relax, so I was going to enjoy this.

Also, I didn't smell so great after our adventure, so everyone around me would probably appreciate my bath, too.

I DIDN'T KNOW how long I was in the bath, but it was long enough for me to fall asleep. Agatha had to shake me awake so I didn't sink into the water and drown. When I got out of the tub, she handed me a cloth to dry myself, then gestured to a brown robe that was draped over the privacy screen for me to wear. It looked just like the one she had.

Once I had it on, Agatha insisted on brushing and braiding my hair. It had been a very long time since someone played with my long strands, so I let her. My friend Pinky had loved to put little braids in, or add colorful hair extensions to match hers. Nothing I would have chosen to do myself, but I had enjoyed indulging her.

A pang of loss hit me in the gut right then, and I wondered if I would ever see my friend again.

Soon I was fully dressed, my braid adorned with flowers. For a moment, I thought maybe they were planning to make me a sacrifice to the adorable, little baby God at the feast. Agatha even put a wreath over Tinker's sweet, little metal head. Afterward, she led us out of the hut and to the feasting area, which was just at the edge of the woods.

Glancing around, I spotted Cade already there, sitting in the circle that had formed around the big bonfire; he too was dressed in one of the brown robes and rope sandals, but he had a wreath around his neck, not in his hair. Although, I suspected he would've looked damn cute with ivy in his luscious dark locks.

His eyes widened as I neared him, and he stood, swallowing. I really hoped that meant my bath and all the beauty pampering Agatha had done was successful. I didn't have a mirror to look at myself, but I felt pretty.

Or at least, I felt clean and knew my skin smelled really good from the flowers in my bath.

"Hi," I greeted him awkwardly. "So, this is all really weird."

He nodded, licking his lips. "You look… pretty."

"Thank you." My hand unconsciously ran over my braid, I liked the way it felt under my fingers.

"The robe, the hair, the flowers… it really suits you."

I leaned into him and waggled my eyebrows. "I do kind of feel Godly right now."

Cade snort-laughed. "I actually do too."

Trying not to be too obvious, I sniffed at his hair. It smelled amazing. "Did they put flowers in your bath too?"

"Yeah."

My eyes narrowed at him. "Did they bathe you?"

"No," he sputtered. "I told them I could do it myself." His cheeks flushed.

"Are you sure? You can tell me, you know? I won't judge you. There was a brief moment where I thought of letting Agatha do it. I mean, she's quite pretty. And also, persistent."

With a shake of his head he turned away, but not before I saw his smile.

The aforementioned Agatha gestured for us to sit

down in the circle, as wooden trays topped with food began to be passed around the villagers. I settled on a straw pad when a tray of purple grapes and papaya was given to me. After eagerly grabbing a small bunch of grapes and slices of the fruit, I offered it to Cade, who did the same.

Honestly, I didn't realize how hungry I was until I tried it, then shoved it all into my mouth, papaya juice running down my chin. There was also a variety of fruits that I didn't recognize, but after the initial hesitation passed, I ate some anyway. If these women had wanted to kill me, they'd had plenty of chances already.

Music filled the area, and I turned to see a couple of women hitting drums, while another couple played melodious tunes on wooden flutes. It was all so surreal that I couldn't stop the stupid grin from capturing my face while I partook in the ancient ritual, whatever it was.

As we ate, Lena joined the feast. Blue stripes were painted across her cheeks and caked in her hair. I knew it wasn't really paint, not the modern kind at least, probably some kind of blue fruit or plant mushed into a paste, whatever they could find out here in the woods. The priestess carried the baby in her arms, still wrapped in the white cloth, but tiny blue marks now adorned its roly-poly hands and feet.

She stepped into the middle of the circle, near the fire, and one of the other villagers handed her a prettily painted wooden cup. It looked quite old. Chanting rose out of the women's lips when she took a sip—words I didn't understand—and Lena poured a stream of the blood red liquid onto the baby.

Realization instantly hit me. It was wine.

I nearly bolted to my feet, wanting to rescue Figgy from being drowned in wine, but Cade grabbed my arm before I could, and kept me sitting.

"It's okay," he assured. "The baby's fine."

"How do you know that?"

"Because that baby is the God Dionysus."

What?!

My startled gaze focused on Lena as she continued to pour wine over him. I had yet to hear a cry from Figgy. In fact, if I listened closely, I could almost hear tiny bubbly laughs coming from the bundled infant.

"Are you sure?"

Cade nodded. "Yes. These women are maenads, and those are satyrs. From what I've read in our history books, they will raise him to adulthood, and be his worshippers. He is the God of Wine and Women after all."

That we were the ones delivering a God to his destiny was mind-boggling. And yet...

"I thought Dionysus was one of the twelve original Gods."

"That's what a lot of people think, and that's what is taught in schools. But the real story is that he was given the seat on the Council of Gods by Hestia, who was the eldest daughter of the Titans Cronus and Gaia."

Taking two of the wooden cups with wine that one of the villagers offered, Cade handed one to me.

"It is said that after the war, Hestia was so disheartened by it and what Zeus did to the Titans—including those who fought by his side, like the Cyclopes—that she gave up her seat in the original God's council of twelve to Dionysus, once he became of age."

I sipped the crimson wine, a hue that should have stained the cup but didn't. Usually, I didn't like the taste, but this one was sweet, full, and delectable, so I greedily took another sip.

"That's crazy." Thirstily gulping the entire contents of the cup, I held it out as Agatha returned with a large pottery jug to refill it. "You do realize I'm going to call him Figgy when we get back to the academy."

So incredibly strange that this baby was one of our teachers. Even with all the incredible things I'd seen since re-entering the world of the Gods, it was hard to comprehend.

"I know." Cade laughed as he too held out his empty cup.

We ate, drank, and even danced around the flickering orange bonfire a time or two after Agatha insisted, until the sun went down, the giant ball of pulsing light sinking heavily into the shadowy tops of the trees.

Tinker even joined in with the musicians, adding some soft bleeps and bloops in time to their lively, unique music.

Tipsy from the sweet wine and exhausted from the day's events, my limbs finally grew heavy, and I nearly fell into the fire. Cade snatched me back at the last minute, and it was declared time to retire for the night and get some sleep. Agatha ushered the both of us to one of the rustic huts on the edge of the thick, verdant woods.

We both stumbled inside, and upon seeing that there was only one bed, we both nearly stumbled out of it. Too tired and drunk to care, I collapsed onto the surprisingly soft, grass stuffed pad and quickly rolled onto my side, tucking my hand under my head. Still, I was incredibly aware of Cade, standing on the other side of the bed.

"I'll just sleep on the floor," Cade offered after a couple of uncomfortable seconds.

"Don't be stupid. Just lie down." I patted the empty spot beside me on the mattress. There was plenty of room for him. "I promise I will contain myself and not try to jump you or anything." I snorted. "You're cute and all, but not irresistible."

"Fine." Stumbling over to the bed, he crouched and rolled onto his back beside me.

I could feel him purposely sliding to the edge inch by inch, so he wouldn't accidentally brush up against me. It made me wonder what he was so afraid of that he couldn't just lie beside me and go to sleep.

CHAPTER FOUR

CADE

*G*ods, she smelled good.

Nicole's scent tickled my nose as I laid next to her on the sleeping pad on the floor. The delicate flower smell on her hair and skin enticed me. Roses, apricots, and something sweet like vanilla. She smelled good enough to take a bite.

And she looked good, too. The delicate, flowing robe she wore suited her, and the way Agatha had braided her hair with intricate twists and woven plaits. Nicole looked like one of them—a Goddess. A Goddess with a wicked sense of humor and mischievous sparkle in her eyes.

She'd teased me about being afraid she was going to jump on me if I got on the bed with her, the joke plain on her face. In reality, it was the opposite. I was afraid I was going to succumb to the myriad of thoughts and feelings I was having about her right now. Warmth, affection, need, desire. Feelings I had no business having, considering what had happened between us in the past.

Unfortunately, I couldn't help it. I liked this Nicole, who had suddenly appeared at the academy. I liked her a lot more than I could ever have imagined. In lots of ways, she was the same. In the way she looked and sounded, the quirky way she smiled, but in others she was different.

She was definitely tougher and had more confidence than before. Nicole had become a badass, and I had no doubt that she could handle herself in pretty much any situation. It pained me to think of what she must have gone through after expulsion, to forge that steel inside her very bones.

I'd had a lot to drink though, and so had she—that sweet, addicting wine sliding down our throats like juice. Agatha had made sure that our cups remained full, so I didn't even know how much, exactly, either of us had had. We were in an exotic, foreign place far from home, removed from time, with the scent of crackling fire and seductive smoke in the air, and the taste of sweet papaya and other unknown fruits on the tongue.

Maybe here, I could forget everything that had happened. If it was possible anywhere, this silent cabin in the trees was it. Perhaps we could just be Cade and Nicole, a couple of people who had just met. Two people who made each other laugh, made each other fall, and made one another vibrate with sexual tension.

Enticed by the thought, I rolled over onto my side, my movements slow so as not to disturb her, and stared at the back of her head, admiring the intricate braids she hadn't taken off. Willing her to roll over, too.

"You're not going to sleep, are you?" Her voice was soft, slightly slurred, and really sexy.

It was rare for the new Nicole to let her guard down, so I was all the more drawn to her in this moment, because she was letting me in.

"Nope."

She rolled over to face me, tucking her hands under her chin. The posture made her look really cute, but I didn't think she'd be appreciative of it if I said so, so I held my tongue. "Let's… talk then, until we fall asleep."

I'd hoped she would suggest something else, but maybe she was saving us from making a mistake we would most likely regret in the morning, when sober and alert. Knowing that didn't stop my mouth from going dry when she shifted and I smelled the flowers she'd bathed in, though. Lucky flowers.

"Tell me about your friend, Pinky," I encouraged, remembering one of the names she'd mentioned to me. Anything, to get her talking, so I could focus on her voice and not on how much I wanted to touch her skin.

That was the right question, because her face lit up with joy. "She's the sweetest person you could ever meet. Kind too. I'm not sure I would've survived on the streets without her."

A rush of fiery anger coursed through my being. What Zeus had done to Nicole made me so mad. He just threw her out to fend for herself. Gods could be selfish, though, and I doubted that many—if any—of them had considered looking beyond her punishment to the ramifications of it. That, I thought, not for the first time, was a distinctly human trait.

"I'm sorry that happened to you."

She shrugged. "It's fine. It doesn't matter anymore. Besides, it wasn't all bad. I met Pinky and some other really awesome people. I learned a lot about myself. I got stronger. And smarter. And very creative in how to get money for food and stuff."

Her lips twitched up into a lazy grin, and I had to

stifle the urge to reach out and trace the curve of her mouth with my finger.

"What did you do?"

"Some odd jobs, but mostly I used to pickpocket."

Eyes widening, I gaped at her, jolted out of my battle with myself. "You did?"

"Yup. I was good at it too." She lifted her hands and moved them around in front of my face, wiggling her fingers with exaggerated motions. "It's all a sleight of hand. Quick fingers. Misdirection."

Nicole tried to tweak my nose, but I caught her hand before she could and brought it down to the bed, pressing it lightly into the soft mattress. I didn't let go of it though. I didn't want to.

"I can't believe you were a thief." I chuckled, painfully aware of the physical connection between us.

"Hey, it paid for food and rent on the crappy little flat I shared with Pinky and Claudia."

"Did you ever get caught?" I didn't like the thought of that, of people who would feel entitled to do whatever they wanted with her for stealing, not seeing that she'd been doing it to survive.

She nodded. "A couple of times." An uncomfortable look crossed her expression. "I stole from the wrong guy once and Claudia paid for my mistake. So, I stopped pickpocketing and got a job bussing tables at this hole in the wall pub. My boss, Raj, was cool though. That's where I started to figure out that I had some weird powers. I saw that girl, Melany, and Hades on TV while working there."

"I think you're amazing for doing all of that. Brave too. I mean, the rest of us came from our family homes to the academy, where we've been taken care of. None of us have had to fight for food or for a bed to sleep in."

I must've said something right, because her smile returned, and she didn't quite look so haunted. "I guess I haven't thought about it like that."

"You're a survivor, Nic. I'm in awe of you…"

I hadn't meant to say that, not in that way, but it was true. I was awed by her, stunned. Not only with how tenacious and tough she was to survive living on the streets of London, and to find her way back to the academy against all the odds, but just with who she was. Right here, right now.

Keeping her gaze captive, I inched my face closer to hers. For a brief second, I thought she might pull back, but she didn't. Nicole held still, swallowing, her eyes shifting down to my lips to track my forward progress. My heart slammed against my ribs as I lightly licked my lips, then inched even closer to hers. We were a breath apart, when a series of bleep and bloops came from the darkened corner of the hut.

Nicole started to laugh, full, hearty bubbles of laughter. "Oh, my Gods! I totally forgot he was even here."

Sighing, I started to laugh as well. "Is there a problem, Tinker?"

"No, there is no problem. I did not mean to interrupt your... conversation."

"Maybe you should turn off for the night."

"That is a good idea. I will turn off to conserve my energy. Good night, Cade. Good night, Nicole."

"Good night, Tinker." Nicole chuckled.

Shaking my head, I rolled over onto my back again. Maybe it was a good thing that Tinker had intervened, and I had a slight inclination that he knew what he was doing. Unable to stop it, my gaze returned to Nicole. She'd also rolled onto her back to look up at the thatched roof of the hut.

Her lips twitched up into a smile when she noticed that I was looking at her. "Tinker has impeccable timing."

"That he does."

Her chest rose and sank with a long sigh. "So, what was it like at the academy after I was expelled?"

"Boring." I chuckled.

"I'm serious." She rolled onto her side again.

"Well, it was chaotic at first." I rubbed at my fore-head. "There were a lot of rumors flying around about what happened. After it settled a bit, we all finished our trials and were placed in our God's clan."

From the way her eyes narrowed, I realized she didn't know what I was talking about, and I had to remind myself that she no longer shared the same knowledge I had. Her memories had not conveniently returned to her.

"We're all connected to one of the Gods. It all depends on our affinities to the elements and our powers. I, like you, have an affinity to fire and metal, so I am part of Hephaistos's clan. You would've likely been placed there too."

"Once you became part of his clan, what happened?"

"For some, they continue to train in those elements, getting stronger and more skilled but Hephaistos offered me a position in Olympus. He said it was so he didn't have to do the work there anymore, but I had a sense he thought it would be good for me, to help me move on."

"Move on from me and what I did, you mean."

I swallowed, hating the pain in her voice, however much she tried to mask it. "I guess, in a way."

"And Iris went to live in Olympus too? You mentioned it before."

For a moment, I paused, unsure of how much information I should divulge about Iris and what she'd gone through afterward. I wasn't sure Nicole was in a place to hear it right now, and I, selfishly, didn't want to tell her.

Not now. Not when we were together like this. Easy, and lazy. To be honest, I didn't want this night to end. In this place we were time travelers, and I desperately wanted to stop time right here, right now. Part of me even wondered if I could use the pocket watch, like she had during the archery training with Lucian.

"She went there to heal," I finally answered. "Chiron is a great healer, but even he has his limits. She got the best care in Olympus."

Slowly, Nicole nodded. "Well, that's something, at least."

"We don't have to talk about it…"

"No, I think we should. I have to at some point, so why not now? Maybe I'll forget about it again when I wake up in the morning with a bad hangover."

Her lips quirked into a small smirk, and I interlaced my fingers with the hand that I had yet to let go of, squeezing it.

"Did she suffer any permanent damage?"

My gut constricted with her question, because I didn't want to answer her, but maybe it was best to get it all out into the open. "She still has facial scars."

Nicole's eyes instantly brimmed with tears, and she blinked back a few, then rolled over onto her back, wiping her eyes. "The one memory I do have of her is that she was quite beautiful. I guess I ruined that."

Unfortunately, I couldn't offer any words of comfort to her. The fire had melted Iris's skin and hair. She'd received a lot of godly potions, tinctures, and powerful spells, but nothing could restore her natural beauty. Iris had begged and pleaded with every God and Goddess to help her, but no one could snap away the damage the flames had done.

Still, I wasn't about to tell Nicole any of that. It wouldn't help matters. It wouldn't restore her memories nor bring her any kind of solace. It would only hurt her, and despite everything she'd done in the past, I didn't want her to hurt anymore. She couldn't fix Iris any more than anyone else could. I knew I couldn't, and I had tried my best for a long time.

"It's in the past, Nic. Going over it won't do you any good."

"It makes sense, though. Why you didn't want to lie down next to me in this bed." Her gaze went to our joined hands, and she lifted them. "I mean, it took a lot of alcohol for you to even want to touch me."

With the words, she tugged her hand out of mine, and my chest burned in response.

"You are right, we don't need to talk about it. Let's just get some sleep, so we can figure out how to get back to the academy, and back to reality."

A certain heaviness fell over the room when Nicole turned over again, giving me her back.

I wanted to reach and touch her shoulder, tug her back toward me. Yet, I knew that despite my warring feelings inside, it would've been a bad idea… for both of us.

We both needed to move on with our lives, however that looked.

First, however, we needed to open the watch and figure out what Tinker had done to activate a time portal, and transport us here. That would be the first challenge. The second one would be how to get us back to our time.

What if we opened another portal and it took us even further back? I had no desire to see a T-Rex up close and personal.

CHAPTER FIVE

NICOLE

*W*hen I woke up the next day, Cade was already out of the hut. So was Tinker. I wanted to think that it was because he was allowing me to sleep in, but it was likely because he was embarrassed about what almost happened between us last night.

Maybe he even regretted it.

As I laid there, staring up at the thatched roof, I tried to decide whether I was glad that Tinker interrupted us or not. My head said it was a good thing, but my heart didn't agree at all. Actually, my heart was a bit pissed about it.

At the same time, what happened—or didn't happen—seemed like a hazy dream. One of those I would almost remember if I could only find the right thread to pull, but the longer I concentrated on it, the further away it floated.

I rolled off the sleeping mat and got to my feet. Wiping my eyes of sticky sleep, I drew back the curtain over the doorway of the hut, and stepped out into the already hot sun. It beamed high in the sky, so I assumed it was nearly afternoon. Perhaps I needed the sleep, because I didn't think I'd slept this long in over a year.

It occurred to me then that I should have had a headache, or maybe some nausea, from the previous night's wine. Instead, I felt pretty great. Sucking in a deep, restorative breath, I cupped a hand experimentally in the air. It felt thick, alive with energy. Maybe there was some kind of magic here that kept illness—and hangovers—away.

I wandered over to the fire pit—where it seemed that the villagers took their meals—and passed a couple of the maenads with handwoven baskets, and pottery jugs similar to the ones that held last night's wine. They were obviously doing their daily chores. They both nodded to me as I continued my way. My eyes found Cade and Tinker at the pit, along with Agatha, Lena, and Baby Dionysus, who was waving his fat fists and gurgling happily.

"Hello, Nicole," Tinker greeted with a joyous beep. His excitement at seeing me showed in the short burst of vibration.

"Hey, Tinker." My hand tapped him on the top of his metal head affectionately.

"Did you sleep well, Nicole?" Agatha asked.

"I did, thank you." I shot a quick, sidelong glance at Cade before I replied. I *had* slept well, better than usual, and I was pretty sure it was because he had been beside me, warmth radiating from his skin to my own.

Accepting the roll of soft bread and some plump figs that Agatha offered, I took my first bite of the bread and groaned at the delicious taste. It was still warm, with a tantalizing yeasty scent, no butter needed. The sweet juice of the ripe fig ran down my throat as my teeth sank into it, and I savored it, thankful to be putting more than wine in my stomach.

I might have felt way better than I should have after all the wine, but I still had a body, and so, I was feeling pretty thirsty.

Cade had yet to look at me, or acknowledge my presence, but I brushed away the burst of annoyance and plopped down right next to him—on one of the firm cushions laid on the ground. I refused to let last night's awkwardness affect us. It was stupid considering we needed to work together to find a way to get home.

"How did you sleep, Cade?" I asked, nudging his knee with my own.

Lifting a hand to his mouth, he cleared his throat and glanced at me, looked away, then dragged his gaze back. The fact that he was being so awkward was almost adorable. Almost. "Ah, good. Thanks."

"Let's not make this weird, mate." Gathering a handful of fruit seeds, I tossed them into the fire, where they sizzled as the flames consumed their moisture. "Come on. We know each other too well for that."

His brows furrowed. "I'm not being weird."

"Okay, good." I stuffed the rest of the bread into my mouth, sad that it was now gone. "Cuz I was starting to think maybe you were going to be all stupid about last night."

"Nothing happened last night." His voice was rough.

Me thinks the gentleman doth protest too much.

"I know. Proves my point though, right?"

He shook his head, but he finally cracked a wry smile. "You're kind of impossible."

I smiled smugly and shrugged. "It's my speciality."

"Since you have helped us," Lena interrupted, gesturing to Baby Dionysus, "How can we help you get... to where you are from?"

Taking the pocket watch out of my pocket, I considered my answer. "I'm not sure. Do you know someone who knows about watches here?" I said it in jest, as we were three thousand years in the past, way before someone invented a working clock.

"Yes, I know this." Agatha nodded, pointing to the watch.

Brow furrowing, certain I'd heard her incorrectly, I held it up toward her. "You know about watches? How is that possible?" After I said it, I winced, realizing that my words made it sound like I thought she was stupid.

"No. I know about time." Standing, Agatha wiped her hands briskly on her thighs, clapping them together before she gestured for us to follow her. "Come with me. I will show you."

Instantly, we stood to follow her, but Tinker hesitated—his gaze going towards the baby Lena held. He shifted, a little back and forth roll of anxiety that she must've noticed, because she brought him closer to the little robot.

"Do you wish to see him before you go?" she asked.

When happy bleeps escaped Tinker, Lena lowered

Dionysus so he could see him. Tinker's pincer-like hand lifted toward the baby, and a chubby little arm popped out of the bundle, wrapping tiny fingers around it. Excitement burst out of Tinker, a series of small beeps, and I swore the baby nodded, as though he understood what Tinker was trying to communicate.

It was so damn cute that I nearly made an "aw" sound.

After Tinker's sad farewell, we all followed Agatha through the trees and into another clearing. In the middle of it sat a sun dial, similar to the one we had in the garden at the academy, but theirs was also wholly different. It wasn't a round stone slab but hemispherical, meaning it was half a sphere, with the pointer on top, and twelve Greek numbers sloped along the edge.

"Did you construct this?" I asked her and she nodded.

"With help from the Goddess Hera."

Frowning, Cade leaned toward me. "How is this going to help?"

I shrugged. "I don't know, but it's worth a look." Curious, I dragged my fingers along the smooth stone, over the numbers, then noticed other small carvings near the twelve numbers at the edge. "What are these markings?"

"The symbols for the twelve Gods."

My intent gaze studied them, trying to decipher which symbol belonged to whom. A flame was depicted on number seven, must have been Hephaistos, and I saw a lightning bolt on number twelve for Zeus. I thought for sure he would've been number one, instead the carving of a sun was found there.

"Apollo," Cade confirmed as my fingers drew over it.

"Why isn't Zeus number one?" I'd asked Cade, but it was Agatha who answered.

"He is on the number twelve because it is the most powerful of numbers. It is when the time of day changes. It is the barrier between day and night."

"She's right. Twelve is a very significant number," Cade agreed. "There are twelve hours in a day and a night. Twelve months of the years. Twelve zodiac signs. The units of time, like seconds and minutes can be evenly divisible by twelve. Even other religions use twelve to mark significant events."

"Okay, so how does that help us?"

He shrugged. "Not sure."

I took out the pocket watch again and studied it. Narrowing my eyes, I squinted at the tiny numbers around the face and discovered something I hadn't noticed before. "Are those symbols just behind the numbers? Like, are they burnt into the metal?" Lifting it, I held it before Cade's eyes.

His brow furrowed as he took the watch from me, squinting too. "It does look like that. But I never put them there when I crafted the watch for you."

"Did Hephaistos help you? Maybe he did it."

Considering it, he appreciatively turned it in his hand. "He did supply me with most of the parts."

"He must have then." I shook my head, still eyeing the watch. "I wonder why I never noticed."

"It's not easy to spot. I didn't either, and I worked with it for days while I put it together."

Once he gave it back, I opened the back to look at the gears and the mechanisms that turned the second and minute hands. "Do you think that's what Tinker did? Somehow moving the hands to point to a special combination of symbols, and that brought us here?"

"Maybe." Taking the watch with renewed curiosity, he inspected the symbols. "What combo do you think would get us back?"

My attention shifted back to the markings on the sundial, several combinations ticking through my brain. Maybe the cornucopia for Demeter, the Goddess of the Earth, the Hearth and Home. Definitely not the helm representing Hades. Possibly Apollo and Artemis, the sun and moon?

Before I could make some kind of guess, Tinker snatched the watch from Cade. "Let me see."

Horrified, both Cade and I reached for the robot before he could do more damage. Our hands touched him at the same time, and instantly, a whooshing feeling gripped my stomach. He'd opened the portal again, and we were sucked through it swiftly. To where, however, I couldn't even predict.

After a few seconds in darkness—at least I thought it was only a few seconds—we landed, for lack of a better word, in an empty alleyway.

Trying to get my bearings, I glanced all around us. We stood between two buildings made of stone with old looking walls. The ground beneath us was also stone and I could hear lively music coming from both openings of the lane. It was definitely not morning or afternoon, but evening. The sun was quickly setting.

"Where are we?" I asked.

"I have no idea. Somewhere in Europe, judging by the architecture of the buildings, definitely not the Americas."

Definitely not home, either.

"What time period, do you think?"

Puzzled, he shook his head. "Hard to say from this back street. The music definitely reminds me of an older time."

"Okay, let's go out quickly and quietly. Tinker, you stay behind us." I started down the alley to our right, and the closer we got to the opening, the louder the music became. A cacophony of voices danced in the air, some even cheering and laughing. It sounded like a party, maybe a celebration of some sort.

When we got to the end of the alley, I peered out of it, finding a massive and buoyant crowd of people. They walked along the street in colorful costumes and masks, a rainbow of flower petals crushed underfoot.

From where I stood, the origin of the music was clearly visible. A band with drums, a violin, and wind instruments was set up on a stage at the edge of a vast city square. Beyond that, dancers in wild, elaborate costumes filled the space, along with street artists performing juggling and magic tricks.

"It looks like a carnival."

Cade joined me at the mouth of the alley. "We're definitely in the twenty-first century." He pointed to a group of girls taking pictures and selfies with their cell phones.

My attention honed in on them, and I heard French dialog swiftly spoken. "We're in France." Lifting my nose to the air, the briny tang of the ocean drifted into my nostrils. "On the coast," I assured, glancing at

Cade over my shoulder. "Could we be in our time period, just in a different country?"

"I don't know." He shrugged. "We should find out."

With a firm nod, we stepped out into the square, and I stopped the first person that went by me—a large woman in a rainbow-colored dress and a lot of pink feathers in her hair. "Excusez moi?"

"Oui?"

"Quel jour est-il?"

She frowned, but answered nonetheless. "C'est le dix-sept fevrier."

"Quelle annee?"

She snorted and looked around, as if expecting a camera man to pop out and say surprise. "Deus mille dix-huit."

"Merci."

Grabbing Cade's arm, I pulled him away from the lady—out of ear shot. Tinker rolled along behind us. "It's 2018."

"Damn it."

I looked around again at the frivolity and the spectacle. "Why are we here?"

"Who knows? Maybe it was just an accident." His glare fixated on Tinker, who had the presence of mind to shrink into himself.

"I did not do anything," Tinker defended. "Nicole was the one who moved the hands on the clock."

He wasn't wrong, but I wasn't about to admit it. "Maybe it's just random. Why does there have to be a reason?"

"I don't know, but the thought of this all being random kind of makes my stomach sick. Because if it's all random, there is less of a chance of ever getting back to the academy. It will always be the luck of the draw, or in this case, the turn of a gear."

As we continued to walk through the square, unsure of where we were going, a darkness spread across the cobblestone. I looked up, toward the pier just beyond a few buildings ahead, and noticed thick, dark storm clouds rolling in from the water. The little hairs on the back of my neck rose. It didn't look like a normal storm.

A couple of screams broke through the music, along with a multitude of voices. Everyone around us froze in their spot when another set of shouts echoed from the pier. Cade, Tinker, and I ran toward the noise. Just as we neared the boardwalk overlooking the water, waves crashed over the embankment, soaking the unlucky observers.

A few people pointed toward the turbulent water,

exclaiming something in French. I didn't understand the words but heard the fear in them.

I followed their line of sight, and nearly swallowed my tongue.

A monstrous form, as high as twenty feet, with horns and scales chopped through a wave almost as large. They headed straight toward the shore, and the people lined up along it, gawking.

CHAPTER SIX

NICOLE

"What is that?" I had to shout over the sound of the crashing water onto the pier. Salty droplets speckled my skin, reaching all the way to where we were standing.

"I'm pretty sure that's the Titan, Oceanus." There was horror in Cade's voice.

Another huge wave surged over the boardwalk, swallowing up a few people who'd been watching what was going on in horror. It pulled them into its greedy, dripping mouth, and then they were just gone, lost to the moving wall of water.

"We need to help those people!" My legs started to

run toward the water, but Cade snatched my arm and pulled me back.

Before I could yell at him about it, he pointed to the sky.

"This isn't our fight, but theirs."

When I gazed in the direction of his finger, I found two people flying toward the monstrous water beast. They both had black wings, but one of them had blue hair.

"Holy shit, that's Melany!" I watched in awe as she dove into the sea and rescued a man from crushing death, scooping him into her arms like he weighed nothing at all. "And who's that with her?" I squinted to get a better look at her companion, who was clad in black and carried a black sword. "Is that Hades?"

Cade nodded. "They were a couple."

I gaped at him. Melany? And Hades? Together? How cool, and kind of hot. "Really? That's so wicked."

"Is it though? I never understood why she fell for him. He seems like a bit of a dick."

"Are you kidding me? The God is smoking hot, and so bloody cool."

I cast him a sidelong glance, still keeping an eye on the enormous battle. It didn't feel right to just stand there, doing nothing while people were dying, but I knew that Cade was right. This wasn't our battle. We weren't even supposed to be there. "You are not jealous of him, are you?"

An irritated huff left him. "No, of course not."

Honestly, I could understand why. I mean, as I watched Melany and Hades battle the Titan with their dark swords, their movements so in sync that it was clear to anyone with eyes that they knew each other intimately, I was a bit jealous. They were both so fierce. I would never be like that. I wasn't a fighter, at least not like them.

"Should we help them battle Oceanus?" I asked, bouncing on my toes. Every cell in my body screamed that it was wrong to just remain there, watching like it was just a movie.

Cade's head shook vehemently. "No. We can't interfere. This already happened. They already won. If we interfere that might change, and then we could inadvertently alter the entire course of history."

"Then why are we here?" If we weren't supposed to help, then I was anxious to move on to wherever we were meant to be.

"Well, that answer would rely on the assumption that we aren't here randomly," he replied in a matter-of-fact manner, then shrugged as an afterthought. "I don't know.

In the ocean, the Titan opened its muzzle, revealing

rows of razor-sharp teeth, and roared. The unnerving sight of the water as a living creature sent a shiver down my back. Both Melany and Hades charged at the beast undaunted, though, Melany issuing a bloodcurdling war cry. Hades swung his sword, and the blade struck the Titan's dripping bicep.

His renewed roar surprised me, but this time it sounded like it was in pain. Assuming a creature made of water could feel pain. I didn't know how they were able to hurt the Titan when it seemed impregnable. However, something must've worked, because there was a shift in the air, and suddenly, it looked like Melany and Hades were winning the battle.

After a few more swoops toward Oceanus while swinging their swords, it appeared Melany cut off a part of the creature, the slice of her blade removing something gold. Instantly, the Titan stopped advancing on the pier.

If I didn't know better, I would have sworn that Hades had a heated conversation with the Titan, making the beast turn and recede back into the depths of the sea.

Within moments, the tsunami-like storm ended, and the surface of the ocean became creepily still. With Oceanus gone, Melany and Hades flew toward the boardwalk. Melany's free hand shoved blue strands back, out of her sweaty face, the other still held her sword.

Cheers and cries of relief erupted from several people who had stayed behind, watching the battle instead of running away like they should have—considering there had been a giant monster trying to kill everyone.

Chances were half of them had stayed to record it on their cell phones, because Gods knew that getting that viral video was worth risking their lives. I couldn't help but roll my eyes. Humans could be so stupid. Myself included.

When Cade grabbed my arm, we retreated into the shadows, into the crowd so we wouldn't be seen. As we moved back, my gaze scanned the throng of people still milling about, their curiosity getting the best of them. There had to be a reason we were there, I was sure of it. I refused to believe this was all random. More importantly, I didn't want it to be.

Like Cade had mentioned, the thought that we could quite possibly not get back to the academy in our own time, made my stomach roil. It made me think of the old Star Trek episodes I would watch with Claudia once in a while. Those characters were lost in space, but Cade, Tinker, and I were lost in time, and it was an incredibly unnerving sensation. Especially, since I didn't know what that would mean to our future.

If we didn't return, did that mean I wouldn't see him when I—or at least me in the past—finally figured out where I was from, and returned to the academy? I mean, three years ago, I would've been in London, living on the street, trying to survive. Though I would've met Pinky by now, I think. It was insane to realize there was another me existing right now in another part of the world.

It was all very confusing, so I shook my head, trying to clear it.

My gaze caught two other people trying to fade into the background and shadows, away from prying eyes—like we had. Those two, however, were very much impossible to ignore.

The woman had long, blond hair, perfectly coiled to the side. Her features were sharp and angular, like a high fashion model. She wore a gold gown that dragged on the ground behind her, and though I knew it was a festival and everyone was dressed in costume, something told me that was her usual attire.

The man who accompanied her was ripped; he looked like a military general, ready to fly into battle at any moment. His arm wrapped around her waist in a very protective manner, and I sensed that guy would kill for her. Maybe he already had.

"I'm pretty sure I just spotted a couple of Gods hanging around in the shadows, and watching the whole thing." Pulling on Cade's arm, I gestured to where I'd just seen the couple.

"Who?"

For a second, I hesitated, unsure, cursing my mottled memory.

"From what I read in the research I did before coming back to the academy, I'd have to go with Aphrodite, and Ares?" I answered. "Do you remember if they were here during this battle?"

Slowly, he shook his head. "Not sure. Melany only gave a quick account of the event, from what Hephaistos told me. But it wouldn't have surprised me. That was Aphrodite's golden rope that Melany cut off Oceanus. She and Ares were the ones releasing the Titans from Tartarus and using them to create chaos."

That baffled me. Nowhere in the news reports over the last years had there been a mention of that. Though, I guess I hadn't paid that much attention, because I'd been concerned with surviving. "Were they responsible for the fire in that forest too? I remember seeing it on TV. That's where I first saw evidence that you all existed."

"Yup, they released a chimera into the forest. If it hadn't been for Melany, Lucian, and the others, a lot of people would've died." Cade frowned disapprovingly.

"Wow. What a couple of dicks."

Cade snort-laughed. "Yeah, that's putting it mildly."

"Maybe they are why we're here."

He looked at me thoughtfully. "I don't know, Nic."

"We should at least attempt to figure that out," I insisted, bouncing on my toes.

"What do you suggest? We can't just go over there and ask what they are doing here, and what it has to do with the Corpse King. They're gone in our time. They wouldn't even know that the Corpse King exists."

"We could just eavesdrop like regular people." I arched an eyebrow as I cast him a sidelong glance.

"I'm pretty sure they'd see us. And they'd recognize us. I know you don't remember, but we were both students of theirs."

Damn it, I didn't want to admit defeat. This had to be the reason; I needed it to be. Sighing, I tried to think of what to do, but my brain was tired. I took a step back and ran right into Tinker, he'd been parked right behind me.

A soft bleep left him. "I am sorry, Nicole."

"It's okay, Tink. It was my fault. I should've checked to see where I was stepping."

"No, I am sorry. I've recorded ten different occasions that I have been right behind you, and you've bumped into me. I should know better." He bleeped.

My eyes narrowed at him. "You record things?"

"Yes, I record everything. You installed a recorder in my operating system."

"Have you recorded conversations we've had in the past?"

He was silent for a moment. Then he seemed to shrink into his little metal shell. My little robot with all the feelings.

I patted him on the head. "It's okay if you have."

"I am sorry I didn't tell you." He was sad.

"It's all right. You can make it up to me right now."

Cade shook his head, already anticipating what I was going to say. "How the heck is Tinker going to be able to sneak up on a couple of Gods? They'll recognize him from the academy too, for sure. It's not like there are regular people walking around with a robot that can communicate."

"He doesn't need to get close. He can record from a long distance, I assume." I glanced down at Tinker. "Right?"

His little dome head bobbed up and down swiftly.

"We just need to get him close enough." Grabbing Cade's hand, I tugged him forward. "C'mon. Before they fly away."

We rushed down the boardwalk to the place where I'd first seen them. I quickly spun around, searching the surrounding area for any sign of where they went. Then I spotted the back of something golden, it glinted in the moonlight, so I pointed.

"There. They went that way."

"Okay, let's follow them discreetly. If we're seen, I don't know what they'll do. Neither of them are—er, I mean, were—very friendly. You won't remember this, but Ares knocked me out of the air during a training exercise. When I landed, I broke my ankle."

A flare of anger instantly bloomed inside me. "What a bloody wanker!"

Cade chuckled. "That's exactly what you called him that day."

Laughter escaped me too. "Good. I'm glad I did that."

We moved across the cobblestone road and around one of the old buildings nearby. Aphrodite and Ares were huddled together in front of a café that was closed for the night.

My back pressed against the wall of the building, keeping me in the shadows with Cade and Tinker. I gestured to the cluster of bushes that sat near us, right beside a public trash can. "That's a perfect spot for Tinker," I whispered. "But how do we get him there without being seen?"

"I got it." Cade's hands began to rotate and the shadows surrounding us seemed to undulate in response to him. "We learned how to manipulate darkness and shadows. I'm not great at it, but it should be enough to cloak Tinker so he can roll over to the bushes."

After a few more twists of his hands, Tinker was obscured in a black haze. I could barely see him through it.

"That's super cool," I admitted, shoving my hand into the thick shadows over Tinker's head. It was cold on my skin, like putting your hand into a freezer for a second.

"You okay, Tink?" Cade asked our robot.

Thankfully, he didn't make a noise, but just nodded his dome.

"So, you know what to do, right?"

Without answering, he rolled out from around the building, slowly inching toward the perfect hiding spot. It was odd watching the small cloud of darkness slowly drifting down the street, like rolling black fog. To the untrained eye, he wouldn't be noticeable at all, but I was hoping that the Gods were so wrapped up in whatever they were discussing, that they wouldn't notice him either.

I didn't realize I was holding my breath until Tinker reached the spot beside the trash can, and I let out a long relieved huff of air. Now, we just had to wait and hope that he was able to record some useful information. It was a long shot, but I refused to just give up.

In silence, we watched intently as Aphrodite and Ares talked. It was definitely a serious conversation as Ares gestured a lot with his hands, and Aphrodite looked perpetually pissed off. Her head suddenly turned, and she looked right toward us.

In a panic, and without thinking, I pushed Cade against the wall and kissed him.

It was as if fireworks went off in my body, and I swore to the Gods that an electrical current sparked from my lips to his.

Eyes wide, I pulled back, panting for breath. "I'm so sorry! I didn't know what to do. She was looking over here and, I thought—"

Cade's hands cupped my face, and he kissed me back.

CHAPTER SEVEN

NICOLE

M y heart slammed hard against my ribs as we continued to kiss. Our bodies pressed together tightly, so close that it felt like the heat we generated had melted us into one.

Cade's back was still against the stone wall of the building, letting me take control, which I was sure was on purpose. I was equally sure that Cade could feel my heart race against his chest. My pulse quickened until my blood was thundering through my veins, and I felt dizzy from the sensations that were overwhelming me.

I didn't know how long we were like that, pressed together against the dusty brick wall, a few minutes maybe, a lifetime. Time seemed irrelevant now, like it had swallowed us whole, but Tinker's soft bleeps from beside us finally broke us apart.

Breathing hard, I scrubbed my hands over my face, and stumbled back a little to get some space. My lungs eagerly sucked in much-needed air, but I resented it because it was fresh and clean, and it didn't contain the heady scent of Cade.

Startled, my attention shifted down to Tinker, then over to where Aphrodite and Ares had been. They were gone. Long gone. Obviously long enough for Tinker to roll back across the street toward us.

I risked a glance at Cade, and saw he too was breathing hard as he rested against the wall. His gaze met mine, showing the conflicted emotions swirling in his eyes. Although, I imagined our emotions were slightly different, but still centered around the same conflict. Iris.

The reminder pulled at me, trying to suck me down from the high I still felt from having Cade's body pressed against my own.

"I did not mean to interrupt your lip meeting," Tinker offered after a few seconds of awkwardness. "I returned to your location after Aphrodite and Ares flew off, just as you instructed."

His comment about what kind of meeting we had

made me giggle, and I let it out freely. Bending over, I laughed harder, bracing my hands on my knees as I snorted with laughter. It was a hilarious way to describe what had just happened between Cade and me, especially when the quaint phrase was uttered in Tinker's oh so polite, ever so apologetic little robotic voice.

After another few seconds, Cade also started to laugh. The sweet sound gave me relief, even as I wiped my eyes, which were running because I'd laughed so hard.

Cade was too serious sometimes. A lot of the time, and I didn't want this unexpected event, no matter how mind-blowing and earth-shattering it had been, to ruin the friendship we were starting to build again—against all the odds that had been stacked up against us.

"Let's hear what you recorded, Tink," I instructed, catching my breath and standing up straight.

Turning in Tinker's direction, I listened carefully as he played back what he'd captured. There were some beeps and whirrs coming from inside his metal body, then two clear voices flared through the little speakers that sat a few inches below his eyes, acting as his mouth.

"That insolent girl is proving to be more of a problem than expected," Aphrodite seethed. Her words were sour, but her voice was sweet. Seductive. Even the recording made me want to reach out and touch her. It was a dangerous weapon.

"We could just kill her," Ares offered, his tone so nonchalant it was off-putting to say the least. It was also clear that to him, killing a human was the equivalent of a human stepping on an ant. He probably thought of humans as bugs.

Cade must've heard it too, because we shared a look of disgust at how easily the God talked of murdering a young woman in cold blood.

"And face Hades's wrath? I think not." Aphrodite huffed.

"He's not that powerful." Finally, a hint of emotion tainted Ares' voice, and the emotion was rage.

Aphrodite laughed, the sound throaty and mocking. "But he is, my love. He is more powerful than Poseidon, and almost as much as Zeus. We would not win against him."

"What do we do about her, then?" Ares was impatient, eager to sweep this pesky girl, whoever she was, out of his way.

"Be patient, and wait for a moment where her demise can be advantageous to us. We will find a way to make it look like an accident." A pause. "What we've come to, when we have to find ways to hide killing a human."

There was a long pause. "Look at that. Young love." She huffed derisively. "How revolting."

That must've been when Aphrodite turned her head and saw us. My gaze met Cade's and we both flushed, each of us knowing exactly what it was she had seen.

"I should've known she was going to be trouble from the first day of training," Ares sneered, grumpy. "I would've orchestrated an accident right there and then, before she gained her powers. Before Hades claimed her."

"Yes, well, neither of us can control time. Only Cronus has that power." The sound of shuffling followed, obviously they were moving about, then I heard the powerful whoosh of wings. The recording stopped after that, and Tinker tilted his head up toward us, hopeful.

"Well, that didn't tell us anything." Cade sighed heavily, raking a hand through his thick hair as he pushed away from the stone wall. "Especially not how to get back to the academy."

Considering it, I frowned. I wasn't so sure. They did mention time, and Cronus. How it was connected to our situation and the Corpse King, I didn't know, but I wasn't going to discount it. Not yet anyway. Not when something in my gut told me that what we'd heard was important.

"And here I thought she was supposed to be the Goddess of Love." I snorted, remembering the sweetness in her voice. It had affected me, but it had also seemed hollow. Saccharine. Like a packet of Splenda instead of real sugar.

"She's more like the Goddess of all the emotions that love can evoke, like jealousy and contempt." Cade's voice was slightly bitter, and I eyed him curiously.

"You don't sound like you have a high opinion of love, Cade." I meant for the comment to be flippant, unserious, but I couldn't stop the question in my voice.

His eyes observed me for a long moment, then he shrugged. "Love is complicated."

Oh mate, that's the understatement of the century.

"We should get off the streets and find a place to crash," Cade suggested.

Briefly, I surveyed the street. It was quiet there, shadowy, away from the main town square, the festival, and all the excitement and horror that a gigantic Titan trying to flood the town had caused. Small cafes and boutique shops peppered the boulevard, all closed for the night, which lent a slightly eerie air to our surroundings.

Still, there were also a few stone townhouses and apartment blocks. Lights twinkled in some windows while others appeared pitch black. It wasn't late, so the dark windows made me think that the homeowners weren't home. Some were probably out for the festivities that the carnival offered, but others might be just plain gone. Out of town for work maybe, or a holiday. Regardless, it was an opportunity of which we could take advantage.

Once decided, I gestured to the place closest to us that had dark windows. My gaze narrowed as I sized it. "Doesn't look like they're home."

Cade looked at me funny for a moment until what I was actually saying hit him. What I was suggesting that we do. "We're not breaking in."

"Why not? We need to find a place to crash, and no one will know. We'll leave in the morning. It's not like we're going to rob them blind or anything."

I wasn't about to admit that I'd done that before as well. It definitely wasn't something I was proud of, but I wasn't sure how Cade would react. To be honest, I didn't want him to think ill of me, especially not when my lips still tingled from his electrifying kiss.

He rubbed his face. "I don't know, Nic…"

"Trust me. I know what I'm doing." Was good at it, even. Sad but true.

"You've done it before?"

"Loads of times. I just find a back window that's open—most people don't lock the small bathroom windows—I slip in, then come down to the front door and let you inside it. If everything is locked up, we move on to the next one. Believe me, we will find a place with an open window."

His hands dragged down his face again, but then he let out a resigned sigh. "Okay, but at the first sign of trouble we run and figure out something else."

"Agreed."

We didn't have to walk far before spotting a place I thought was definitely vacant. Thankfully, there was a lovely, little walled garden separating it from the neighbors and the main street. The homeowners obviously wanted their privacy, and it was a perfect set up for someone like me to break into it.

"Can I get a leg up?" I asked Cade.

Nodding, he linked his fingers so I could settle my foot on them, and lifted me. My hands gripped the top of the stone wall, and I hauled myself over until I was easily able to straddle the wall.

"Be careful," he whispered, and I gave him a saucy grin.

"Of course. I'm like a ninja." And the funny thing was, I was like a ninja. I could climb walls like

Spiderman and leap long distances like the Hulk, maybe not over tall buildings but a girl had to have lofty goals to fend off boredom.

I jumped down into the small, secluded garden, and eyed the side and back of the townhome to look for a good entry point to try. First, I tested the balcony door, not expecting it to be open and found it locked. Then I tried the back door, for good measure. Also locked. No surprise there.

My neck craned when I looked up the side, spotting a small window on the third level. It probably belonged to a bathroom with a shitty lock, or no lock at all.

A trellis was bolted to the wall, there for the ivy that snaked along the wooden structure, so I began to climb it until I could reach the nook in the stone. It made for a great handhold, and I was able to continue using the different notches in the wall, finally reaching the small window.

Hanging on my left arm, I reached up to the window with my right, and nudged the glass. At first, it didn't give, so I thought maybe I was going to have to break it, but I kept pushing on it and the pane thankfully swung inward.

It took a bit of upper body strength, but I managed to pull myself up and shimmy through the opening. Setting my hands on the sink, so I didn't land with my head on the floor, I finally made it inside the townhouse.

It was a small thing in the grand scheme of things, but it gave me a lot of satisfaction. I didn't like relying on other people for my survival. Not even Cade. Especially not him; I didn't want him to think I was weak. He should know that I was fully capable of taking care of myself and had for the past three years.

What the academy had given me and cruelly snatched away when I became inconvenient, was not something I needed.

Thankfully, I'd been right about the window belonging to a bathroom. My eyes traveled around the small room that had a toilet and sink, but that was about it, so I stepped out into a small bedroom.

Back in the day, it had most likely been the servant's quarters, but now it was a kid's bedroom. Judging from the plethora of sequined blue pillows, blue netting over the bed, and the knitted, mermaid tail blanket on the bed, this room belonged to a teen or young girl. The urge to flick on her under the sea nighttime lamp stirred within me, but I tamped it down and left the room.

Quietly stepping out of the room, I stood on the third-floor landing, straining to hear any sound that meant someone was home. After I counted to thirty in my head, and didn't hear anything but a ticking of a clock somewhere and an old furnace, I smiled, satisfied. It was safe, so I quickly descended the two levels and went to the front door to unlock it for Cade and Tinker.

Before I could reach the doorknob, Tinker rolled out from the darkness of the hallway. "Hello, Nicole."

I jumped, a little squeak of surprise escaping my lips.

Cade stepped out next to him. "Sorry. Didn't mean to scare you."

"How did you get inside?"

"Tinker insisted on picking the lock."

"And you couldn't stop him?" I gave Cade a scathing look.

He shrugged. "He wanted to test his skills. Besides, he kind of whined about it."

My glare shifted down to the little robot, although he wasn't who I was pissed off at to be honest. "Why didn't you tell me you could pick locks?"

"You were so adamant about finding a window and breaking in that I did not want to disappoint you. You seemed excited about the prospect of it."

I really hated that he was right.

CHAPTER EIGHT

CADE

*A*fter Nicole had calmed down from being startled by us lurking in the foyer, we wandered into the kitchen to find some food, not inclined to be picky. Both of us were starving, and we also needed to find an outlet to plug Tinker. He needed energy too.

I dreaded the thought of being stuck in some era long enough where he ran out of battery power. Thankfully, I had installed some solar panels, so if worst came to worst, he could still power himself with the sun.

Opening the freezer, Nicole immediately found us

some frozen dinners that we could heat up in the microwave. They were probably going to taste like cardboard, but it was the best solution. There were no perishables around anyway. Obviously, the family had planned on being away for more than a few days.

After our dinners were cooked, we took them and sat on the kitchen floor, behind the island. Nicole explained that it was best to keep out of sight even inside. We couldn't turn on any lights either, so I created a small globe of warm yellow light to keep us company as we ate our dinners. It wouldn't be seen from the street, even if someone was deliberately looking through the windows.

"Jumping from full day to night is jarring, and I know that technically we've only been awake for no more than eight hours, but I'm still exhausted," Nicole admitted as she yawned, leaning back against the island.

"Time traveling is like having permanent jet lag." At least, I thought so. I wasn't sure I'd ever experienced it.

A chuckle left her with the last bite of the chicken pot pie that we both had chosen to eat. "I'm pretty sure I spied some ice cream in the freezer. Do you want to share a tub?"

"What kind?"

"Does it matter? It's ice cream, duh." Nicole snickered.

"Yes, it matters," I countered with a smile. "I draw the line at pralines and pistachio."

"Mate, both of those can be enhanced with the right sugary details. I mean, pralines and caramel is quite good, as is pistachio with almonds."

"Nope, no nuts in my ice cream."

"No buttered pecan or maple walnut either?"

I shook my head.

"Not even peanuts? Are you actually telling me you'd say no to a huge scoop of Rocky Road?"

"Yes, I am actually telling you that." I couldn't help but grin at her outraged expression. She was clearly offended on behalf of tree nuts everywhere.

"I sure am learning a lot about you on this crazy trip." Her head shook like she was sadly disappointed in me, but I knew she was playing. "What is your favorite flavor, then?"

"I like the classics. Chocolate and vanilla. I have also enjoyed chocolate chip cookie dough…"

"Oh, thank the Gods!" Laughter escaped her. "There's hope for you yet."

"But my favorite is probably butterscotch ripple."

Her grin widened. "Guess what's in the freezer?"

My eyes narrowed even as I smiled. "You're lying. There's no way."

Scrambling to her feet, Nicole opened the freezer and took out a big tub of butterscotch ripple ice cream. After she grabbed two spoons from the cutlery drawer, she plopped back next to me on the floor. With a wide smile and her eyes twinkling with warmth and humor, she handed me one of the spoons then held hers up, clinking it against mine with a dramatic flourish. "Cheers!"

It was right then that I realized how much I'd missed Nicole, and why. She was one of the warmest and most loving people I'd ever known. In the past, she'd effortlessly made me laugh and feel good about myself. She still did that. That hadn't changed about her, even if other things had.

While we ate the ice cream, we talked about everything but our current situation. It was nice, a break. Like two regular people hanging out and getting to know each other.

She told me about all the places she liked to hang out in London with her friends, and her enthusiasm made me ache to visit them all with her. I wanted to see them through her eyes. In turn, I told her about growing up in a small town in Canada, which she said sounded like something out of a sitcom.

"Do you have siblings?" Curiosity captured her voice as she dug her spoon into the ice cream.

I nodded, feeling a slight pang where my heart thudded in my chest cavity. "A younger sister."

"What's her name?"

"Grace."

"Do you miss her? Do you miss your family?"

Sadness clouded Nicole's gaze with the mention of family; she had no recollection of hers and I felt bad that I couldn't help her with that. She had never talked about them since we first met.

"Yeah, I miss them."

"Do you get to see them now that you've 'graduated' from the academy?"

"I saw them once. Hephaistos let me go back before I went to work in Olympus."

"How did you get there? I mean, that's a long way to fly." She snorted.

"I used the portal to Canada. It's in the lake at the academy and you come out through the falls in Niagara Falls."

"No way! When you got your Shadowbox, were those your instructions, to go through the falls?" When wonder colored her expression, I knew she was picturing the majestic, beautiful, and incredibly powerful tourist attraction.

I nodded, barely suppressing a shudder. "I had to jump into them."

Her eyes widened and she gaped at me as though she couldn't imagine hating that. Of course, knowing her, she would have loved the experience of looking down the thundering fall of water and then jumping in to become part of it.

"What? That's crazy." Tsking, she shook her head. "Man, they really do a number on you, don't they?"

"What do you mean?" My brows furrowed while I ate another spoonful of dessert.

"The Gods." Licking the left over ice cream off her spoon, she got to her feet, and placed it on the counter. "They make you jump through all sorts of hoops. Then punish you if you don't. They're cruel."

I stood, and leaned against the counter next to her, setting down the now empty tub and my spoon. "Yeah, some of them are. Zeus definitely was. Aphrodite and Ares, too. But Hephaistos, Dionysus, and Demeter… they're good. Since Prometheus took over the academy, things have been better."

"I guess, since I have no way of knowing." She shrugged.

The urge to pull her into my arms, soothing her pain and discomfort about the past rushed through me. Instead, I awkwardly patted her on the shoulder—like an idiot. Maybe I should hang out with Hades, learn some of his cool moves since Nicole thought he was sexy. Though, knowing me, what looked epic on him would seem ridiculous if I did it.

Nicole pulled away then, shrugging off my ham-handed attempt to comfort her, and tossed the now empty ice cream container in the trash. Our garbage was something we would have to deal with when we left. I didn't think we should leave any proof that we had been there. Other than the pilfered food, of course, which I felt bad about, but it couldn't be helped.

"I'm tired. I'm going to go lay down in one of the beds." She cast me a quick glance, and I knew she was thinking about how we'd both slept last night, close enough to feel the warmth from each other's skin.

"It's probably a good idea that we both get some sleep." I wanted to feel her warmth next to me again, but I wasn't sure how to ask, or if I even should.

Nicole nodded, and after making sure that Tinker was still good, we went up the stairs to the second floor to choose bedrooms. I told her to take the master bedroom with the king-sized bed, but she chose the second bedroom instead, which appeared to belong to a teenage girl—judging by the looks of the band posters on the walls, and the fairy lights strung up over just about everything.

Saying good night, she went into the room and shut the door. Considering opening it back up and just hugging her close, I set my hand against the door for a moment. Maybe even swallowing my awkwardness long enough to suggest that we should sleep side by side again. For safety's sake, of course. But I chickened out and crossed the hallway, walking into the other bedroom.

I didn't shut the door though.

Now I lay awake on the king-sized bed, staring at the ornate ceiling in the bedroom where I'd chosen to get some sleep. Honestly, I should've been thinking about how to get the watch to work, what we were going to do if we couldn't get the portal to take us back home, instead I was thinking about the kiss we shared. My lips tingled with the memory... as did other parts of my body.

Sitting up, my hands scrubbed my face. I should never have let it happen, despite the fact that I'd wanted to kiss her since the day I saw her in the garden. Sure, I'd tried to deny it, but I hadn't gotten over her. Which was crazy, considering I hadn't even realized that I had a thing for her to begin with. It took seeing her again to have all the conflicted emotions come flooding back, like the tsunami that Oceanus had created only a few hours ago.

With a heaved breath, I got off the bed and crept down the hall to the bathroom. Once inside, I ran the cold water and splashed it over my face. I was kidding myself thinking I was going to get any sleep. Not with the feeling of Nicole's lips still on my mine, her smell ingrained in my nose, and the sensation of her silky hair in my hands. Nope. Those thoughts were not conducive to a restful sleep.

Going back downstairs, I sat down next to Tinker. He was currently in sleep mode while charging, and I didn't want to wake him. It felt rude to, so I took out the pocket watch and studied it. It was killing me that I couldn't figure out how the time portal was opening.

What were we pushing or turning to make that happen?

It was most likely a combination of things, but I couldn't see the possibilities clearly. That was infuriating, considering I'd created the damn thing.

One thing was for certain though, all three of us had to be touching it. At least, I was pretty sure, yet that was something I wasn't going to try testing. It was too dangerous. One of us could be left here with absolutely no way to get back. Still, one of the constant variables had to be the connection between all three of us.

Fueled by intrigue, I opened the glass encasing the

clock face, and inspected the symbols etched above the numbers. It was crazy to me that I hadn't noticed them at all when I put the watch together. That was something I was sure I should have seen while working so closely, and with a magnifying glass no less.

Unless they weren't there to begin with, but that meant they had magically appeared in the past few days. Or maybe they had been activated somehow by using the watch. Perhaps Tinker had triggered them when he first messed around with it in the Hall of Learning. If so, that confirmed these glyphs were the key to determining how to open and travel through the time portal.

Nicole had moved the clock arms to the ones that represented Aphrodite and Ares, and that was who we had encountered. Although we had yet to determine the importance of the information they divulged, I still didn't like the way they'd so casually discussed murder.

Examining the symbols, I attempted to decipher a code that would get us back to the academy. Who represented the academy? The lightning bolt for Zeus maybe. He had been the founder of the school along with Prometheus.

There was no symbol for Prometheus, so maybe Hera? They were, or had been, the power couple of the academy. Except, they weren't there anymore. Did that mean we would travel to the school, but arrive when they were still alive? I wasn't sure that would be helpful to us.

My gaze went to the fire glyph for Hephaistos; maybe his was the code for home. The Forge God was like a father to me since the beginning of my training, although he would be aghast to hear that, and I would never tell him.

Nicole also had a strong connection to him, even if she didn't remember it all. He would deny it vehemently, but I was sure he had a soft spot for her. From what I'd heard, Hephaistos had also connected to Melany when she was at the school.

For being known as such a curmudgeon, he sure had a penchant for the misfits, those who didn't seem like they belonged. Perhaps that was how he felt as well. As though he didn't truly belong to the council of the Gods.

I knew that was how Nicole had felt at the academy. Like she didn't belong. She'd always compare herself to Iris, who had been her roommate, and I suspected that Iris had also been her bully.

Nicole never came out and said it, but sometimes I'd notice the way Iris looked at her. It wasn't always friendly, and if I finally admitted it to myself, I'd also seen some of Iris bullying. Her snide and disparaging remarks about her to others, always within Nicole's earshot. Unfortunately, I'd ignored it, looking the other way, which made me culpable.

Thinking back on it, I wish I'd done something then, said something. Then maybe the incident on the obstacle course would never have happened and Nicole wouldn't have been expelled from the school. Then none of this would have occurred.

My hand lifted, fingers tracing my lips. Then I wouldn't have the feel of her on my lips still, and in my hands. When I sucked in a deep breath, the enticing scent that clung to Nicole in the forest returned—roses, apricots, and sweet vanilla.

As I thought about our kiss again, the scent in my memory shifted, growing an acrid note. Smoke. Was it real or in my head? I got to my feet and moved toward the front foyer. The smell was stronger there. My gaze went up the staircase to the second floor.

Nicole.

CHAPTER NINE

NICOLE

*A*fter I shut the door on Cade, I knew I wasn't going to have a restful sleep. Speaking about the past wasn't pleasant, especially when it had to do with a past I didn't remember. It was frustrating and pissed me off.

The fact that other people had memories about me that I didn't, made me feel powerless. It was like they knew things about me that even I didn't know about myself. They did, really, because how could I be my entire self if I couldn't remember the events that had shaped me?

I could follow that thought process around in

circles, and it was absolutely maddening. I wished Cade could understand how upsetting it was, and how much I hated the Gods for betraying and abandoning me. Deserved or not, it was cruel.

Maybe Hephaistos and the others didn't have a hand in it, but they didn't stop it either. It might have been unfair of me to put that kind of expectation on them, but hey, I figured I had a right to be angry and unforgiving. I mean, I'd been just a dumb, confused kid who didn't know any better, and they were Gods.

It made me think of the recording Tinker had gotten, of Aphrodite and Ares. Of Ares's chillingly empty voice as he discussed killing someone, and the arrogance in Aphrodite's sickeningly sweet tone.

They were the Gods, all of them, and I knew that my punishment likely didn't register much in the grand scheme of their immortal lives, if at all. Still, that didn't make what they'd done right. If they had so much power, didn't that mean that they had a responsibility that came with it, a commitment to help those of us who were less powerful?

Wishing I could turn on all the fairy lights to give me some comfort, I sat on the bed. Their little bits of sparkle would remind me of Pinky. However, I knew I couldn't turn on any lights, the last thing we needed was to be discovered here. Getting arrested would be the worst possible thing to happen to us. They'd separate us from the watch and we'd never get out of this time and place.

Plus, what would happen to Tinker? They might take him apart. Find out what made him tick. Study him to gain the knowledge to make more. The thought sent a dread-filled shiver down my back.

Yawning, I laid back on the mattress, plumping one of the many furry pillows behind my head. So tired, yet not at all sleepy. There was a bit of a chill in the air, so I grabbed the edge of the blanket and pulled it over me. It was an old house, so it didn't surprise me. Actually, I liked it, it reminded me a bit of my flat in London. All damp and creaky.

I rolled over onto my side and closed my eyes, hoping for sleep to arrive. For a moment, I thought about calling Cade to come and lay down beside me, but to be honest, I wasn't sure that would've been conducive to sleep either. Not when the thought of kissing him against that stone wall sent a ripple of pleasure surging through my body.

Frankly, I wasn't actually sure I could control myself if he laid down beside me again. It wasn't smart, but now that I had tasted him, I knew that I would forever crave to taste him on my tongue once again.

I pushed that thought down, deep down where things that could never happen lived. It wouldn't do us any good to have our emotions get the best of us. We needed to focus on how to get out of here.

Another yawn escaped me, and I rolled onto my back. If I was going to get any rest, then I needed to think about something else—or stop thinking altogether. Maybe trying to puzzle out the past couple of days would help. Unfortunately, thoughts of the Corpse King gripped my mind before I finally drifted to sleep. That turned out to be a huge mistake.

My surroundings changed, and although I knew it was a dream, I had no control over what happened.

At first, I was wandering through a mass of gray mist so thick, that I couldn't see anything in front of me or behind me. It appeared like I was walking on a cloud, although I knew instinctively that there was ground beneath my feet. It felt like a cloud too; the air on my face was cool, wet, and dense, leaving a sheen of chilled moisture on my skin. There had to be water nearby.

I kept moving, although it sort of felt like I was on a treadmill, going nowhere. After a few more minutes, or what I perceived as minutes, a thunderous noise cut through the air. Startled by it, I jumped as it echoed all around me, bouncing off something solid.

Extending my hand; my fingers brushed against a hard surface. It felt like rock, firm and cold beneath my touch. My fingers came away wet as well.

Where was I? In a cave maybe? I sniffed, detecting the scent of humidity, the metallic scent of rock, the must of still air.

My location soon became apparent as the mist slowly dissipated, revealing a stone tunnel. Thankfully, a source of light shone ahead, and I wasn't encased in darkness. I was definitely in a cave, and now I realized that the deafening sound that invaded my ears was the crashing of running water. Perhaps a waterfall nearby, hence the dripping water along the rocks.

When I approached the opening from the tunnel, the darkness gradually lightened. I saw flickering light from torches, and the moving shadows of whomever was in the cave. My heart slammed against my ribcage as I stepped into a cavern and saw the last thing I'd ever thought to see again. The undead, scurrying about mechanically, doing only the Gods knew what.

A few of them carried shovels. Were they digging inside the cave? Was that even possible? The ground beneath my feet felt solid like rock.

One of them stopped what they were doing and turned my way. I froze, waiting for it to attack, a reflex. Spinning on my heel, I ran back to the opening of the tunnel but when no blow came, I realized that they couldn't see me. Remembering this wasn't real, nothing more than a dream, I turned back to observe what they were doing, invisible in their midst.

The few with the shovels marched into another section of the cavern, the clanging sound of their blades hitting stone reverberating as they tried to dig into the solid ground. They grunted and groaned, making other inhuman noises that set my teeth on edge, and the hairs on the back of my neck to rise.

My interest peaked when I heard another sound, but it also made my stomach roil. I knew deep down what it truly meant.

I followed the sound of hooves clattering on the stony ground, and came around the bend to find the Pegasus tied up to a stake protruding from the floor. Its ears flickered when I neared, and it whinnied as if it recognized me. It was then that I realized, that quite possibly, I wasn't actually in a dream. Or that I was, but somehow, some way, the dream was real.

"You!"

My body spun with the call, to see The Corpse King ambling across the cave toward me, his skeletal finger pointed in accusation. It rattled as he shook it.

Shit. This wasn't a dream. This was real.

"How dare you come here?!" Reaching down to his waist, he drew the huge broad sword strapped there.

In a panic, I whirled around again but discovered there was no escape. He stood between me and the way out. I was quick, I could run and duck, but I didn't know if I was don't-get-hit-by-the-long-sword quick. I'd never had a reason to test that in my banishment, and I wasn't sure if I should even take the chance. So, my only other option was to fight back, but I didn't have a weapon.

Well, I didn't have a weapon like a sword, a knife, or a gun, but I wasn't completely helpless.

Fisting my hands tightly, little sparks of fire shot out from my fingertips. I guessed I did have a weapon, just a really unconventional one that may, or may not, actually work in my favor. Only one way to find out, though.

Concentrating on bright fire and flickering flames, they swiftly manifested into red-hot tendrils, swirling around my clenched fists. When I opened my hands, two fireballs the size of grapefruits formed in the curve of my palms. Rearing my right arm back, I threw the fireball at the Corpse King as hard as I could, aiming right for his head.

I was pretty sure I'd surprised him with my sudden attack, because he didn't think to duck out of the way, and the flaming globe hit him in the side of the face. Flames erupted over what little flesh was left on his skull, and he let out the most blood-curdling scream I'd ever heard.

Not waiting around to see anymore; I made a dash for the exit that was behind him. As I ran past him, he blindly swatted a hand at me. His fingers caught a chunk of my hair and he yanked me backward, making me land on my ass on the stone floor. I immediately scrambled to my feet to get away.

"*Nicole!*"

It was Cade's voice. Was he here in the cave too? If he was, I couldn't see him.

When I tried to run away again, my head was yanked back. Damn it! I couldn't let the Corpse King stop me. I had to get out of there. Pulling my hair out of his grasp, I felt a few strands rip out of my scalp. The pain was immediate, and it radiated all over my head and face.

"*Nicole! Wake up!*"

Strong hands gripped my arms and I spun around in a panic, thinking the Corpse King had grabbed me, but he was shrieking and patting at the fire on his face.

"*You started a fire! We have to get out of here!*"

Immediately, my gaze fell to my hands to find the flames whirling around them, like tiny tornadoes.

Trying to put them out, I flicked them, but the fire wouldn't go away.

Then there was a sharp sting across my cheek…

I opened my eyes.

Cade had me by the arms and was ushering me out of the bedroom. Thick black smoke swirled around us, and I couldn't see much beyond it. It filled my nose and mouth, making me cough. Looking over my shoulder, I saw that the bed I'd been sleeping on was engulfed in flames. The blazing force eating the blankets and pillows, turning them into blackened char and ash.

"Put this over your nose and mouth." Cade handed me a small tea towel he must've gotten from the kitchen. I did as he instructed, then he pushed me out of the room and into the hallway. "Get downstairs and get Tinker! Get out of the house!"

Before I could ask him what he was going to do, he started to pull and grab the air in front of him. I didn't know what he was doing until I felt small drops of water on my cheeks. He was extracting water out of the air to douse the flames.

It seemed to be working a little, some of the flames had stopped crawling up the walls, but there was still a good-sized fire on the bed. Dropping his arms, Cade shook his head anxiously, and then backed out of the room.

He whirled on me. "I told you to go!"

"I'm not leaving without you."

My hand reached for his, and I pulled him toward the staircase. We both ran down the stairs to find Tinker already waiting for us in the foyer. The faint wail of approaching sirens echoing along the street. Someone had thankfully called the fire department, but that also meant we would have a harder time leaving the house unseen.

"Can you do the shadow thing around us?" I asked Cade.

"I'll try." His hands swirled around, pulling at the corners of the room. I could see the darkness shimmering, but it didn't move like it had before. He kept trying until his hands shook with exertion. "It's not working."

"What else can we do?"

"I don't know. I can't fly all of us out of here. Not before this place is crawling with firefighters and the police."

Before I could offer any other suggestion, the door swung open and Tinker started to roll out of the house. "I will devise a distraction so you can escape."

"No!" We both chased after him, but he was too quick for either of us.

Tinker rolled down the short walkway and out onto the street. Loud bleeping and blooping noises burst out of him, and he waved his metal arms. "Do not shoot. I am unarmed."

It would've been comical if the situation wasn't so dire.

Except, what he was doing was working. The neighbors who had emerged from their apartments watched Tinker roll around like a chaotic trash can, and it gave us a chance to get out of the house. Cade went first while I followed him, running out onto the street without notice.

Soon, it seemed like we were nothing but another couple of spectators. We just had to get Tinker to stop doing what he was doing and meet us around the corner. I tried to get his attention, but he was too busy making a dramatic spectacle of himself.

Suddenly, a fire truck came to a stop in front of the apartment complex, effectively blocking us from reaching Tinker.

CHAPTER TEN

NICOLE

"How do we get him out of there?" I shook my head wildly, my hands balling into sweaty fists. "What was he thinking?!"

"He was thinking about saving us. It's in his nature."

Guilt crumpled up into a ball in my gut, and I swallowed past a sour knot of grief that lodged in my throat. It was my fault we were in this position. Absolutely. I should've known that I wasn't dreaming. A child could tell the difference between reality and a dream. I should've known what would happen when I ignited that fire in my hands.

Like before, I'd lost control. It happened in the cemetery when I'd first encountered the Corpse King, and when I burned Iris in the obstacle course.

Frantic, I surveyed the area, the firefighters were charging into the house, water and foaming fire-retardant roaring through the serpentine coils of the fire hose. Some of the neighbors were now more focused on that than on Tinker, but I could hear the excited voices of some of them as they realized that he was a moving, talking robot, something that wasn't necessarily seen yet. At least not out in public.

We had to act now, before someone with authority got a hold of him and took him away.

"Give me the watch." I put out my hand toward Cade, seized by a sudden and wild idea. When he just blinked at me, I gestured impatiently.

"Why?" His hand covered it through his clothing.

"Well, for one, it's mine. And second, I'm going to use it to stop time so we can get Tinker out of here." I jumped in place, urging him to move faster, to get what I was saying.

Understanding dawned on his face and he shoved his hand into his pocket, pulling out the watch. He gave it to me. "Like back at the academy on the training field?"

I nodded, rubbing a thumb over the watch. "I'll

press the button, and we'll run over, grab Tink, and then get the hell out of here." Lifting my hand, I prayed it would work. "Get ready. One, two, three…"

Cade grabbed my arm, just as I pushed the button.

Everything stopped, so abruptly that it seemed like the whole world had crashed into a giant wall. It felt like there should have been some kind of sound, a roar and a crash, but instead, everything fell instantly silent, utterly still. It was reminiscent of a really dark themed Rockwell painting.

The water spraying out of the hoses hovered mid spray. The flames of the fire stopped crawling along the walls and roof. I was drawn to that, both intrigued and repulsed by the flames, because fire wasn't meant to be still, but I had a far more important purpose.

I took it all in for a split second, before my body caught up with my brain and I made a dash for Tinker, running the fastest I'd ever run in my life. Cade ran with me around the firetruck until we spotted the little robot. His metal arms were frozen in the air—mid-shout.

Swiftly picking him up, we carried him down the street and around the corner. Once we were safely out of sight, I pressed the button again, and time sputtered forward in motion.

"—shoot!" Tinker finished, then his dome head

swiveled around, clearly puzzled. "Oh. I am safe now."

I patted him. "We all are."

For a moment there, I thought Cade was going to make a snide remark like "No thanks to you", or something similar—given the way he was looking at me. I wanted to snap at him, tell him that it was hard to look both horrified and disgusted at the same time, but he was managing it very nicely. That wouldn't be helpful though, so I swallowed my words.

He seemed to as well, and just scrubbed his face and sighed. "Let's find a place where we can have privacy to figure out how to get out of here."

I almost suggested breaking into another house, which is what I would have done if I was alone, but after what just happened, I knew Cade wouldn't be keen. Instead, we found a couple of chairs and an umbrellaed table left out by a tiny café in a narrow back lane.

It was dark and there was no one around, so it was a good spot for now. We needed to take a moment to regroup.

When I sat, I noticed that my hands were shaking, so I shoved them under my legs where Cade couldn't see, and I could get them to stop. "I'm sorry. I, ah… I had a nightmare, and it got out of control."

Reaching for me, he dug out one of my hands from

under my leg. The touch soothed me more than I cared to admit. "It's okay. You didn't do it on purpose. It was an accident."

Guilt still swirled around in my stomach, even as I nodded. Gods. I could have killed Cade. Tinker. Myself.

"What did you dream about?"

"The Corpse King." I cringed at first, then sighed. "But I think maybe it wasn't really a dream, and I actually saw him."

"What? Are you sure?" Cade asked, intrigue shining in his eyes.

"I'm not one hundred percent sure, but it felt like it. It felt real, like the last time." As I said it out loud, I became more certain that the dream had in fact, somehow, been real.

"What did you see? Where was he? Was it, like, in this time, or back in our timeline?"

"I'm pretty sure it was in our timeline, because I saw the Pegasus chained up in a cave."

"A cave?" He frowned.

"Yeah, I was in a tunnel, pretty sure there was rushing water nearby too. The sound was really loud, and the rocks were wet. Then I came out into a large cavern. I saw a bunch of the undead, ghoul guys using shovels to dig into the rock, but they didn't see me."

"Were they mining?" He frowned again. "Rocks? Coal?"

I shrugged, suddenly weary. My adrenaline had crashed. "I don't know. I guess."

"And you saw him?"

"Yeah. And he saw me. Just like the time in the cemetery. He drew his sword to kill me, so I threw a fireball at him. It hit him in the face."

"And that's when you started the fire in the bedroom."

Feeling tears gather in the corner of my eyes, I nodded, and cast a sidelong glance at Tinker. My stomach roiled as sour guilt gathered into a tight knot in the pit of it.

Cade squeezed my hand tighter, lacing our fingers together, and tugged me closer to him. "It's okay, Nic. Don't blame yourself for what happened. You were in trouble and reacted the only way you knew how."

"I thought you'd be mad at me."

He shook his head, giving me a little smile. "I can't be mad at you, I realize."

"Good to know." I sniffled. Damn it, I hated to cry. I wouldn't do it. And yet, I didn't think that Cade would judge me for it if I did.

A few chuckles escaped him. "I think I may have made a mistake letting you know that."

"Nah. I won't use it against you. I promise."

That made him laugh even more.

"Did you have an inclination of where that cave might be?"

I shook my head, disappointed in myself. "No. Could be anywhere, don't you think?"

"Yeah, maybe." Considering it, he turned to Tinker. "Tink, could you run a search on any open mines in Europe?"

"I didn't know he could do that." It pissed me off a bit that I didn't know that either, not unlike how I imagined a mother might feel if they discovered a secret about their child.

"After you were gone, I gave him like a Google type search engine. He's a walking PC now." Cade offered me an apologetic glance, having picked up on my irritation.

A series of soft whirring sounds left Tinker, then he let out an excited bleep. "There are two hundred and sixty-three working mines in Europe."

Cade sighed heavily. "That's a lot of mines to search."

"Yeah. Besides that, we have no way of searching for them, not right now anyway." I tapped a finger on Tinker's head. "What else can you search for? Do you have a browser history?" I laughed, curious about this new thing I didn't know about him.

"Yes, past searches…"

Cade looked really uncomfortable as he pulled back from me, dropping my hand. Oh Gods, I kind of didn't want to hear about any embarrassing things Cade had searched for in the past. That shit was definitely private.

"We don't need to hear that, Tinker."

"Nicole Walker, fifty-five times in the past three years."

Well, that was a big surprise. I gaped at him. "You Googled me?"

He shrugged but wouldn't meet my gaze. "It's not a big deal really. I was just curious whether you'd pop up somewhere, then I would know you were okay."

"Cade," my voice became thick with emotion, "that really is a big deal. You have no idea how that makes me feel, knowing someone was looking for me even when I didn't know who I was."

He swallowed. "I wish I could've done more. I should've done more…"

Before I could let my thoughts talk me out of it with some bullshit rationale, I leaned forward, cupped his face, and kissed him.

When I pulled back, Cade's eyes were wide, staring

at me like a deer caught in the headlights of a Mack truck. "Nic, I…"

"Awwww. I'm so happy for you two!" Tinker blinked his big metal eyes at us, then reached over and set his metal claw hand on Cade's arm…

We were suddenly shooting through a blinding white vortex. A kaleidoscope of colors whizzed by us. If I squinted really hard, I could almost make out images of people and places that then blurred into another, then into another, and another. My stomach roiled from the jittering motion.

It all came to an abrupt, jerky stop, and we tumbled onto the ground in a jumbled heap.

I pushed off the floor, which was white stone, and looked around us. We were on a very narrow walkway, shaded from the sun, and between several houses made from the same white stone too. Red shale covered all the roofs. Cade got up too, glancing around as well.

"Do you recognize where we are?" I asked.

He peered into one of the open windows of the house next to us. A window without glass. "I'd say we are definitely not in the twenty-first century."

The sound of voices neared us, so grabbing Cade and Tinker, we tried to make ourselves small in the shadows of the lane. Two women walked by, chatting amicably. They both wore colored togas and leather sandals, their dark hair piled on top of their heads in complicated twists and braids.

"Shit," I whisper-hissed. "Looks like we're back to ancient times."

"Definitely after the Gods' War though." He pointed to a spot between houses, and I could see a large white building, with columns and big steps. Out front was a huge statue that looked like Zeus in all his mighty glory. "We must be in one of the Greek city-states."

"Do you know which one?"

He shook his head. "Hard to say from here. There were quite a few that had temples for Zeus. Some states had temples for many of the twelve."

"How did we even get here? None of us had the watch."

Cade's hands rubbed his face. "Maybe it's Tinker."

We both looked down at the little robot, but he blinked up at us innocently. "I do not think I have opened a time portal. It is not in my programming."

Perplexed, I surveyed the area, taking in all the historical implications of our destination. "Why are we here? There has to be a reason?"

"I don't know, but we need to change into something else so we're not noticed. I don't suspect the guards here would be very understanding."

"You could just pull out your wings and flap them a few times, then they'd fall to their knees thinking you were a God."

He shook his head. "No one's going to think I'm a God."

It killed me to see how self-deprecating Cade was. He had no idea just how cool he was. Even among all the others at the academy, Cade stood out. He was like a God in my mind.

After we found a couple of togas drying out on a laundry line, and changed into them, we stashed our clothes and shoes in a safe place, as well as Tinker. I felt bad for leaving him, but there was no way he could move around unnoticed.

Cade and I went out into the main square to figure out where we were, and why we'd ended up here, but I found it hard to blend in with the populace. Even though I'd put my hair up in some sorry excuse for a bun, I looked out of place. It was probably my extremely pale complexion. Cade, on the other hand, looked the part of a wealthy Greek man. Almost every single woman, old or young, turned their head as he walked by us.

I was about to point it out as we neared the pantheon, but a tall man with abundant, curly brown hair, and a short beard stepped out of it, standing on the top step to address the growing crowd. He wore a lot of gold, and a crown gleamed on his head.

"Welcome, my people. Today is a glorious day. We are to be blessed by the Gods."

As if to punctuate the statement, a bolt of lightning zipped down from the sky and struck the top step of the pantheon—near where the man stood. A crack of thunder followed, and from the white smoke of the strike, emerged the God of Lightning himself—Zeus.

The crowd gasped at the sight of him. I did too, to be honest. He was even more impressive and formidable standing at the entrance of his temple, than he'd been riding on the Pegasus into battle on the beach.

Instantly, the people dropped to their knees in deference to the God. Cade did as well, pulling me down with him. When in Greece, and all that, I guessed.

"Welcome, Zeus," the man declared with his arms open toward the God.

The look on Zeus's face told me he wasn't all that happy the man hadn't bowed like everyone else.

They clasped arms. "I look forward to the feast, King Lycaon."

"As do I." The man smiled, and it was then that I realized that Lycaon was in fact, the Corpse King.

CHAPTER ELEVEN

NICOLE

*H*oly smokes.

"King Lycaon is the Corpse King," I murmured to Cade out of the side of my mouth. My entire body had gone rigid. I kept expecting the king to whirl, shake a bony finger in my direction, and then try to extinguish my very existence. It was kind of his MO.

Brow furrowed, Cade turned toward me. "Are you sure?"

I cast him a look as I nodded. "Of course I'm sure! I'd recognize that cruel smile anywhere, even with healthy flesh covering his deformed skull. Besides, he's wearing the same crown."

And furthermore… I just knew. Knew it in my bones. Still, I didn't understand what my connection to the Corpse King was, but I knew that it existed, a long silken thread binding us together.

I would bet my life on it, and I was a little bit afraid that I'd wind up having to do just that.

Tall, broad, and regal, Zeus held out his hands toward the crowd. It was an invitation to stand, so we all did, pulled to our feet like puppets on a string—which I supposed we were, because Zeus was a God.

"Come." Lycaon gestured to his people, trying but not quite managing to emulate the charisma of the God beside him. "Bring your offerings to the temple, and we shall all feast together." Turning, he together with Zeus, walked into the temple. His steps were lazy, calculated, designed to show off his statue and power.

Some of the people in the crowd hurried forward, carrying baskets of plump figs, bright red mangoes, and papayas so ripe that their skin had split open, leaking out the sweet, sticky juice from inside and revealing the dark, pearl-like seeds. Others carried trays heavy with baked goods—large loaves of fresh bread, flaky pastries, while the rest carried sweets, glinting with the sweet golden ooze of honey.

The smells made my stomach clench with hunger, until a man walked by with a bleating goat on a rope. I winced, hunger evaporating at the thought of what was going to happen to that poor goat.

"We are going to need something to offer if we hope to get into that temple," I whispered as more people brushed past us to go inside it. They were salmon swimming upstream, and we were merely rocks in their way.

"I don't know what. It's not like we can just run out to the orchard and pick some fruit. And we definitely don't have any farm animals to sacrifice."

"What about Tinker?" I asked, suddenly inspired. I thought about the little robot hiding in one of the back streets.

Cade frowned at me, unimpressed. "What about him?"

"Is there some way we could use him to get entrance? We could say we are great metalsmiths from, I don't know, Athens or some shit, and show them how Tinker can serve people like he did for Dionysus?"

"I don't know, Nic. That would be playing fast and loose with history and science here." He exhaled loudly as he considered it. "That would inspire some really big changes. We'd be exposing them to a technology that won't be invented for thousands of years. Also, Tinker would definitely get noticed by Zeus, and then we'd be changing the course of our history. In the future, Zeus would totally recognize us at the academy *and* Tinker. It would change things. And we don't have any idea what that would mean for the events that have already taken place. Like your expulsion, or Melany and Hades's uprising. Zeus's demise. Our presence could alter all that."

"Well, aren't you a buzz kill." I huffed, but he was right. Of course he was right, and I could see it, but I still didn't have to like it.

He shrugged. "Sorry. You can imagine how popular I was in high school."

That made me giggle, even as I rolled my eyes. "I'm going to say that you probably had NO IDEA how popular you were. I imagine all the girls were mad in love with you."

He didn't answer, instead turning his head to search the crowd, but I caught the slight tilting of his lips. Maybe he did know.

I could just picture him, the tortured soul flitting around the edges of the crowds at a human high school, drawing girls toward him with the charisma that was in his very blood. *Cheeky, mate.*

The thought made me wonder who I had been, or if I'd ever even gone to high school at all. Shaking it off, I followed Cade's lead, glancing along the throng of people amassing around us. They were everywhere.

There had to be a way in for us, a way to blend in with the teeming crowd. This event was why we were here. I knew it deep in my bones. We had to witness it, and then maybe we would know the Corpse King's motives. Because he had some deep-rooted ones, that was for sure.

On the edge of the square, I spotted a trio of people, two men and one woman, who were performing juggling tricks. One of the men lit the ends of a stick on fire, and twirled it around to the amazement of the onlookers. Ha! That was child's play compared to what Cade and I could do with fire.

I nudged him in the side and gestured toward the trio, feeling my fingers spark as I thought about what we could do. "We get in with them."

"As street performers?"

I nodded. "Yeah. I mean, we could swallow fire and they'd think it was a trick."

His fingers rubbed along his jaw as he did some thinking. It was a cute tick of his, but now probably wasn't the best time to think about it. "What if we're seen by Zeus? We can't draw a lot of attention to ourselves, Nic."

"We'll disguise ourselves and blend in with the rest of them." The woman wore a scarf over her hair, so I could find one as well to drape over me and hide my face. "Once we're inside, we can find a hiding spot to watch the proceedings."

After another minute, he finally nodded. "Okay, it's our best bet."

We headed back to the lane behind the houses, to find scarfs and cloak ourselves, then returned to the square just in time to slide in behind the trio—they were making their way up the steps to the pantheon's entrance.

As the performers approached the temple guard, who was granting people entrance, they each did a trick. The woman juggled three apples, while the two men handled the fire sticks. With no emotion, the guard nodded to them, and they were allowed to enter the temple. I wondered if they would have been granted entrance with just their small offerings, if they hadn't been able to do a trick along with them.

Quickly, Cade and I pushed in with the trio, but the guard stopped us with a drop of his spear, glowering at us.

"We're with them," Cade explained.

His brow furrowed as he scrutinized us.

Tricks. They liked tricks. Smiling sweetly, I raised my hands and lit them up with fire, wiggling my fingers. His eyes widened and he flinched back a little. I couldn't stop the grin that blossomed on my face, though I did manage to hold back my laughter.

Nodding, he lifted the spear. "Go through."

With a sigh of relief, I closed my hands to snuff the flames, as Cade and I crossed the stone piazza, entering the grand temple through one of the wide doorless entrances.

The crowd of people milled about in the huge space. Some were at the main altar, depositing their offerings, while the others who had already done their duty, began to eat. Their gazes became affixed on the raised dais, where Lycaon and Zeus sat, at a long stone table piled high with the makings of a sumptuous feast —all for them.

Part of me wondered what they would do with all the offerings. Surely, they had to share, or it would be such a waste. Briefly, I thought of how many times my stomach had clenched with hunger, in the years after I'd been expelled from the academy, and barely managed to swallow past my disgust.

"We need to get closer to the dais," I whispered, trying to shake it off and focus. "We have to hear what's going on."

"You said we were going to find a hiding spot," Cade reminded me.

I made a face, waving a hand in his direction to dismiss his naysaying. "What's the fun in that?"

"Nic…"

"They're talking about something. We need to know what it is. It's the whole reason we are here. To find out about the Corpse King." I gestured to the table, where Lycaon and Zeus were engaged in an intense conversation, and realized it was starting to look strained.

King Lycaon seemed oblivious to the danger of inducing Zeus's wrath, or maybe he enjoyed poking at the God, because he clearly had no plans to stop. The look on Zeus's face was getting darker and darker by the second, and I felt a foreboding tremor course through me.

I grabbed Cade's hand, and pulled him through the crush. I didn't particularly want to be close to either Lycaon or Zeus while their tempers rose, but I did want to hear what had them arguing. Maybe we could hear something that would help us get home, or find out more about the Corpse King.

As we got closer, Zeus's voice rose above the chatter of everybody else. "Where are your sons? You promised me they would be attending this feast."

Lycaon sniffed. "I made no such promise."

"When you prayed at my temple, you asked for all

the power and wealth I could bestow upon you, which I have." He waved his hands around, indicating the temple and the citizens. "And in exchange you vowed to give me the pick of your fifty sons, to take them and train them in my Gods' army." His voice got louder.

More people stopped what they were doing to watch and listened to what was happening. Near the dais, at other tables, I noticed many young men getting to their feet, so I assumed that those men were Lycaon's sons.

"I would never sacrifice any of my sons to you!" The king sprung to his feet, spittle flying out of his mouth.

As Zeus slowly stood, I could feel the electrical energy in the air begin to spark.

The little hairs on my arms and the back of my neck rose to attention. I glanced at Cade, finding he had noticed the shift as well. It wasn't hard to see that something monumental was about to happen. A low buzz of concern rippled through the crowd around us, and a few men and women started to back away from the dais. They were smart to do so.

Instinctively holding hands, Cade and I also backed away. We only stepped to the side though, so we could still see and hear what was happening. My fingers tingled with anticipation, at the possibility of having to use my fire power to protect Cade and myself from whatever horror was going to be unleashed.

"Do you dare break your vow to me?!" Zeus's voice thundered across the temple. The columns holding up the stone roof vibrated ever so slightly.

"I do. I've earned my power and wealth. And no one, not even the great Zeus, can take it from me." Lycaon raised his hand, and from every corner of the pantheon guards dressed in armor and carrying weapons rushed toward the dais. The men at the front, his sons, also drew swords from scabbards secured to their waists.

"So be it." Zeus rubbed his hands together, and the whole temple seemed to tremble.

Cade and I nearly lost our balance. A woman and her child next to us fell to the floor as the ground shook beneath our feet. I reached out to help them stand.

"Attack!" Lycaon yelled, his face going red from the effort.

The guards and his sons all charged toward Zeus, who had yet to move or react. Screams erupted from the crowd, inciting a stampede to get out of the temple, but when they neared the exits, stone pillars tumbled to the ground, effectively blocking their escape.

Zeus's hand swept toward the advancing band of

armed men, and one by one, they were blown backward by an unseen blast of energy. They landed on their backs, asses, or over each other in a heap. Most of them scrambled to their feet to try again, but never even made it a few feet before they became frozen in the spot.

Zeus lifted his hands to the sky, and I braced for the inevitable bolts of lightning to zip through the large open skylight in the ceiling and skewer every single one of these men, but that didn't happen. Instead, every one of Lycaon's sons, and a few of the guards, dropped to their hands and knees—as if forced down by a giant, invisible hand. I realized a bit later that those guards were also his sons.

Beginning to panic, Lycaon tried to run down the steps of the dais toward his sons, but he never made it. He, too, became frozen where he stood. Although even if he hadn't been, I wasn't sure what he thought he could do.

"You are a foolish man, Lycaon. And you will pay dearly for that. You will watch as I curse your sons, and there is nothing you can do to stop it. The only thing you can do is understand that YOU caused this. This is your doing, and you will have to live with it for the rest of your miserable life."

"No!" Lycaon shouted. "No, I beg you! Please do

not hurt my sons. You can take them. You can take them to be in your army."

"Oh, I will take them, but it won't be for my army. It will be for my trophy wall."

My stomach roiled as I watched all the men on their hands and knees start to convulse. Their bodies shook, bunched, and twisted into new shapes. It was horrific, but I couldn't look away from what was happening. One by one, each of Lycaon's sons broke through their human skin and became wolves.

Lycaon's desperate shouts pierced the air as he tried to move down the steps, his body also visibly convulsing, but still couldn't. He couldn't look away either.

I grabbed onto Cade. The look of horror on his face matched how I felt inside. This was worse than anything I could've imagined. Especially, when I sensed the horror wasn't over, and was just beginning.

CHAPTER TWELVE

NICOLE

a great shadow from beyond the domed skylight in the temple ceiling slowly darkened the pantheon, and I looked up to see a huge, winged black horse with crimson red eyes fly overhead. Its inky hair streamed in the wind its wings stirred.

I knew that horse, had seen it in the stables at the academy—a massive, hugely muscled, arrogant beast. Upon its broad back sat the God of War. With a loud *hyah!* Ares steered the horse to the opening so he could dismount and land on the ground inside the temple ground. Foreboding surrounded him like a dark cloud.

As he thundered forward, there was a flash of light

right beside him. It wasn't lightning, but more like a sunbeam explosion that pressed right against the darkness of Ares. From within the bright, glittering white rays, a woman with long blond hair, dressed in an elegant golden dress walked out. She wore a gold chest plate made for war, but it was also ornate and beautifully crafted.

When we'd seen Aphrodite before, she'd been beautiful in a cruel sort of way, but now? Now she wielded her power with a vengeance, instantly reminding all onlookers that while she might be the Goddess of Love, she was, in fact, still a Goddess.

A slow and satisfied smile tilted Zeus's lips with the new arrivals, and the expression made my blood grow cold. "Aphrodite. Ares. Are you ready to go hunting?"

Ares grinned cruelly, then unslung the bow he had strapped to his back. Aphrodite's hand lifted, seeming to fashion a bow from the sunshine that radiated all around her. Zeus clapped, and a bolt of lightning manifested in his grip, followed by the deafening boom of thunder.

My stomach tightened, and I felt sick.

"They're going to kill all his sons!" I clutched Cade's arm, fingers digging into his muscle. "We have to do something."

"We can't, Nicole. We have to let it play out." His

voice was calm, but the muscles of his jaw tensed with the war inside of him, the same one that was inside of me.

"Run, my sons!" Lycaon shouted, his voice contorted through a muzzle of part human teeth, part elongated fangs—the result of being stopped from completely transforming into a wolf like his sons. He threw his head back, letting loose an ululating sound that froze the blood in my veins.

The Gods were both beautiful and terrible to behold. Lycaon was just terrible, a creature so unnatural it shouldn't exist.

There was an explosion of action and sound as all the wolves let out a howl, mimicking their father, and sprinted for the blocked exits. Chaos erupted inside the temple as everyone ran, unable to get out—wolf and citizen alike. Some of the wolves jumped onto people's backs, muscles rippling elegantly as they clawed at the human flesh. They had gone wild in the madness, trying to escape. Human screams mixed with the animal whines and growls, and blood quickly stained the white marble floors.

That was just the start, though, the real horror was yet to come.

Zeus threw a lightning bolt into the crowd, skewering two wolves in one shot. The smell of burning flesh hit my nose as the bolt of pure heat and light pierced them.

"Two down, forty-eight to go," Zeus announced with a bit of a flourish, a cruel smile and wave of his hand directed toward Lycaon.

"No!" Lycaon shrieked, his voice that of a creature not entirely human. "Please don't kill them! Please! I will do anything."

"You missed your chance to do something." Zeus nodded, directing our attention to Ares, who knocked an arrow and let it fly. It struck one of the wolves in the flank, but not before it pierced right through an old man's leg.

The wolf went down, yet he didn't die right away. Lycaon's son writhed and whined in pain on the marble floor, his wildness gone, looking like nothing more than a dog bewildered when his human master abused it.

Beside him, the old man writhed and screamed, clutching his leg, tears running down his gnarled face and soaking his long white beard.

"I can't watch this!" I shook my head, teardrops sliding down my cheeks. "I have to do something." Gripping Cade's hand, I begged him. "Help me."

He hesitated, because we weren't supposed to do anything that could affect the past, but finally nodded.

Together, we ran to one of the blocked exits. There

was a crush of people crammed up around the broken columns, trying to move the heavy stones out of the way so they could get out of there. I spotted the woman and little girl I'd helped earlier. They were both huddled on the ground while hugging each other tightly, bloodied and bruised, their clothing in tatters.

Cade pushed through the masses until he reached one of the stone columns blocking the exit. He put his hands onto the white rock, and I thought he was going to try and push it with his Demigod strength. Instead, he closed his eyes, took in a deep breath, then slowly let it out keeping his hands against the stone.

I wasn't sure of what he was trying to do, but after only a couple of minutes, the column started to crack. Those cracks soon turned into wide gaps, until the entire length of the structure broke apart. The stone crumbled to the floor in small chunks, opening the exit as it rained gravel and dust down on the crowd surging against it.

While people and wolves streamed out of the temple through the opening Cade created with magic, I gathered the woman and her child, helping them get outside. The woman cradled the child against her chest, and I supported them both with an arm around the woman's shoulders.

Once we were out, and I escorted them to a spot

that seemed safe—at least for the moment—I noticed Tinker at the other blocked exit, trying to smash through the heavy stone with a mallet he must've found somewhere. I didn't know how he'd sensed that we were in trouble, but I was so happy to see him.

Cade and I rushed over to the little robot and helped remove the broken column from that exit, Cade working his magic again. More people streamed out, screaming, bloody, and wild. A few had scratches on their bodies from the wolves who had tried to run over them in their franticness to get away.

I knew we hadn't saved them, not by a long shot, but at least we'd given them a fighting chance. Maybe one or two would survive, along with the people. I refused to believe that it was all for nothing. Although, that notion quickly left me as the roof of the temple blew open and Zeus, Ares, and Aphrodite flew out, landing on the top front steps as easily as if they'd stepped from a stone onto the grass.

Knocking a golden arrow in her bow, Aphrodite let it fly. The arrowhead found its mark in the head of a wolf sprinting across the main square, trying to go toward one of the small neighborhoods. Her tinkling laughter rang in the air.

"We haven't had a good hunt in ages." The

Goddess sighed happily, as though reminiscing about the good old days. "This is going to be fun."

Aphrodite was literally the worst. I'd somehow managed to push through the initial appealing of her sparkling voice, and now found it cloying instead, as though her words could drown me in honey.

The urge to charge at her and light her on fire awakened in me, but I knew I wouldn't get close enough to do just that, before she took me down with one of her arrows. I didn't remember her from my academy days, because I didn't remember freaking anything, but I sensed that she was just as horrible in the future as she was now, right in front of me.

A terrible creature, intent only on fulfilling her own desires.

Those people—sorry, those perfectly cruel Gods— were the ones instructing a bunch of teenagers on how to fight and kill in the name of their army. They didn't need our help. They were quite capable of wreaking evil havoc all on their own, and I just about fell to my knees to puke at the thought.

The three Gods took to the sky, kicking off from the stone effortlessly, soaring toward their hunt like a flight of raptors, and leaving the rest of us to pick up the very bloody pieces.

I sunk to the ground, my muscles giving out in the

wake of my utter horror, and put my head in my hands. My fingers gripped my hair, tugging it, hoping the bite of pain would wake me up from what I dearly hoped was just a terrifying dream. "This isn't right. We should have done more. This can't be how it ends."

Cade hesitated, shifting his weight back and forth as he stood above me. Then he sat next to me, putting his arm around my shoulders and drawing me in close to his solid body. With a deep inhale, his scent swirled into my being—metallic and smoky, offering me comfort from how familiar it was.

"I know it feels that way," he whispered. "We can't save Lycaon's sons, but we did save a lot of innocent people. Of that I am certain."

I chose to feel good about that, rather than stress about the fact that we might have changed the past. Yet, I couldn't have seen this unfold in front of me and not done something to help, not if I wanted to stay true to who I was.

Finally, I nodded and leaned against him, resting my head on his shoulder. "At least now we know what the Corpse King wants. Revenge against the Gods for his sons' deaths."

I didn't express it, but I understood Lycaon's motive. The Gods were cruel, immoral, and didn't deserve our reverence of them. There was nothing divine or truly reverent about them. They were just as flawed, maybe even more so than humankind, with the powers to inflict pain and suffering whenever they saw fit.

"Now we just need to figure out how he's going to do it," Cade agreed.

In the distance, Zeus fired lightning bolts toward the ground. Ares had already landed just past the city-state walls. I imagined him running through the sparsely set fig trees, arrow knocked, laughing as he speared wolf after wolf, after wolf. Aphrodite was still flying around in the air next to Zeus, shooting her light arrows.

I clenched my hands into fists to stop them from igniting. Cade must've sensed my fury, because he set his hand over one of my fists and squeezed, forcing me to look at him.

"Let's get out of this city. We don't need to see anything more."

He was right, so I nodded. There was no point in suffering through this. It was a piece of history. It had already happened, and there was nothing we could do to change it. We had gotten what we came for, and now it was time to figure out how to jump out of here.

As we both got to our feet, movement stirred behind us. I turned to see Lycaon shuffling out of the temple, dragging one of his legs. My first thought was that maybe he'd hurt it trying to run down the stairs to help his sons, but on closer inspection, I realized that his leg was twisted and bowed the wrong way. It was a wolf leg, to go with his half-transformed wolf face. When his people saw him, the women screamed, and everyone ran away from him, crying.

Zeus had taken more than his sons from the king. He'd taken his kingdom. Lycaon was an abomination, and no one would bow down to his rule anymore.

I imagined he would be driven out of the city very soon, as the nobles tried to restore order. It wouldn't surprise me if one of those nobles made a deal with Zeus for wealth and power, just as Lycaon had.

The Corpse King turned his head to look at us, and I had a strange but strong urge to go to him, to console him. Despite being a bad king—though I didn't know that for sure, maybe he had been a great leader and his people loved him—he still deserved sympathy for the loss of his sons.

Instinctively, I stepped forward, reaching out a hand toward him. "I'm sorry this happened to you." For a split second, it felt like I was moving faster than everything around me. I had almost touched his hand before he even registered that I was there.

"Nicole." Jerking me out of the trance I almost

went into, Cade grabbed me from behind. "We have to go." He pulled me away from Lycaon and down the steps of the temple. Tinker followed us down.

Thankfully, no one had taken much notice of him, despite his obvious strangeness. They had other things to focus on, like the fact that Zeus and Ares were flying back, each carrying the bodies of a few of Lycaon's sons.

When the Gods touched down, each of them tossed three wolves' bodies into a pile. They landed with a sickening thud. Crying out, Lycaon stumbled down the pantheon steps, and collapsed on his knees near the mound of his dead sons.

Cade's arm wrapped around my shoulders, and he ushered me away from the square. Tinker rolled along behind us. When we got back to the houses where we'd first arrived, Cade found our clothes and tucked them under his arm, leading us through the city and out the main gates—now defenseless. A few houses with fruit trees and other crops scattered across the land that stretched outside the city walls.

"Let's see if we can find a place to rest on one of those farms," Cade suggested. I was too numb to answer him, so he just took my hand and led me down the dirt road.

The first house we came to was occupied, so we

continued to the next one, which sat far from the main road. It was an olive farm. The stone house was fairly big, probably housing three generations of farmers. It seemed empty though, and I imagined the occupants had gone to the city for the big feast.

We went inside, and the first thing Cade did was sit me down on some cushions on the floor and get us water from the basin in the kitchen.

"Tinker, can you stand near the door and be the lookout? Alert us if you see anyone coming down the path."

The robot rolled over the entrance and parked himself there, ever so vigilant.

Quickly drinking the water, I nearly choked on it. It felt like I had sand in my mouth and throat.

Cade's hand slowly rubbed my back. "Take it easy. I'm pretty sure you're in shock."

Once again, he was probably right. I felt detached, but also strangely calm.

He went back to the kitchen and rummaged through the baskets and shelves, then sat beside me with a hand full of crusty bread and some dates. Taking the bread, I chewed on it while in a daze. I knew I needed to snap out of it, but it was all so overwhelming.

In my young life, I'd seen bad things like starvation, a fist fight that put two people in the hospital, and serious drug addiction—the kind that left bruises all over arms and legs. One time, I even saw the dead body of an old homeless lady who died under her rain tarp at night, but nothing had prepared me for the level of violence and destruction Zeus had unleashed.

"I'm going to need you to get it together, Nic." Cade rubbed my back again.

With a deep sigh, I turned toward him. "I'm tired. Why can't you get it together for the both of us? You're smart. You figure out how to get out of here."

"I would, except I'm pretty sure that you are the reason we're jumping through time."

CHAPTER THIRTEEN

NICOLE

"What now?" I gaped at him, sure that he was just making stuff up to get me to snap out of it. A quick slap to the face would have probably been a better strategy, and more effective.

"Well, the last time we jumped we weren't touching the watch, so it's not the watch. Then I thought maybe it was Tinker who was creating the time portals, but thirty minutes ago I saw you move through time, unaided, without the watch, without us. It happened when you tried to touch King Lycaon. You became a blur, Nic. Like you were a train speeding along a station."

Shock rushed through me at his statement. Had I really moved through time to get to the Corpse King?

"You think I'm opening the portals, and sending us to these different time frames?"

"Maybe not consciously, but yes, that's what I think."

"But none of this started to happen until I pushed the button on the watch."

He nodded. "The watch is a focus. It's an item that amplifies your power. Like a witch using a magic wand. The magic is inside the witch, but it is focused by using the wand. I think it's the same thing for you. Does that make sense?"

I got to my feet and paced around the room. "Not really. I mean, why would I send us here?"

"You were thinking about the Corpse King. You had a dream about him, remember? And we were talking about why he was doing what he's doing. You brought us here to answer that question."

"If so, why did I take us to the Gods' War?"

"We were in the hall of learning, reading up on the Gods." Cade shrugged. "It could've been in your mind, or you read about it briefly. Then there was all that focus on the watch from all three of us touching it... and bam. We traveled back three thousand years."

Considering it I shook my head. "I don't buy it.

Doesn't make sense. Why would I send us to France to see Melany and Hades fight Oceanus, huh?"

"You talked about admiring her, thinking she was cool. Maybe that was all it took for your subconscious to direct us there."

Suddenly feeling a lot of stress building, I paced some more. If that was true, how the hell was I going to get us back to the academy when my thoughts were all over the place?

"I don't know, Cade. That's a lot of presumptions you are making."

He stood too. "True. I am connecting some dots that might seem far-fetched, but honestly, it's the most logical answer." His hands closed around my biceps, stopping me from walking and holding me still. Cade's eyes bored into mine. "You are the source of the power, Nicole. I know you think it's the watch, but it isn't. That is just a watch, something to tell time with. I know, because I made it. It's not that special, but you are."

Gods, his eyes were amazing. I wanted to fall into them, to drown myself. To lose myself forever.

Also, I wanted to kiss him, but figured it probably wasn't the most opportune time. We were trying to figure out this time jump thing and get us home. Laughter almost left me at my inappropriate train of thought, but instead, I bit down on my lower lip. I hoped it looked like I was seriously considering his logic, and not thinking about jumping his bones.

"Okay, so what do we do? Test this theory?"

Dropping his hands Cade shrugged. "Yeah, I think we're going to have to. But we really got to do it right. You're going to have to focus your thoughts."

I threw my hands up into the air. "But what if I can't? What if I start thinking about dinosaurs, and send us to the Cretaceous period, and you get eaten by a T-Rex?"

Mouth twitching, he cupped my face with his hands. "That's not going to happen."

"What if *I* get eaten by a T-Rex?" Tinker asked from his perch by the door. His little metal body slightly shuddered. "I know dinosaurs could not digest metal, but it would be awful to be inside its large stomach."

"No one is getting eaten by a T-Rex, okay?"

I nodded.

"Erase that from your mind."

"Okay. It's erased." It wasn't. I was still thinking about it, and it was pretty vivid in my mind.

"Let's all sit down on the floor together. Tinker, come over here." Cade sat, pulling me down with him. We both crossed our legs, so our knees were touching. "Tuck yourself in here, Tink." He pointed to the inter-section of our legs and Tinker rolled into it, so he was touching both of us. Cade then pulled out the watch from his pocket.

"I thought it wasn't the watch," I challenged.

"It isn't, but it will help focus your thoughts." His hands held mine, sliding the watch in between our palms, and he tugged me forward. "Look at me."

So I did, and again, all I could focus on was kissing him.

"Think about the academy. Picture it in your mind."

With a settling breath, I thought about the garden where I first ended up after walking through the flames, followed by the room where I'd been staying. Concentrating hard, I pictured the room in the Hall of Learning, where this had all started. I saw myself sitting in the chair, flipping through a book while Cade sat nearby, also going through a large tome.

A smile curved my lips, remembering how his brow furrowed so tightly as he concentrated, and how I'd wanted to rub my thumb over the creases to smooth them away.

Again, I thought about kissing Cade.

"Can you see it?"

I nodded.

"Think about it. Only concentrate on the academy. Clear away everything else and keep your focus on it."

Academy. Academy. Academy. I kept the mantra going in my mind, silently saying it over and over again.

"Now, imagine us being in the academy."

Once again, I did. Except, I saw Cade and I wrapped up in each other, sitting on my bed. We were kissing, and it was the most perfect thing in the whole world. That's where I wanted to be. In that place, with him. He was my home.

Oh shit! My eyes widened, and I tried to picture something else, but it was too late.

An invisible force pulled my body, and then we were zipping through white space. Being sucked through the portal.

Soon we were falling.

I landed on the hard floor of the library, right on top of several large books that were scattered all over the place. My knee smashed harshly against the leg of a wooden chair. Grunting, I rolled over onto my back, cradling my knee and blinking up at the painted dome ceiling of the Hall of Learning.

Holy shit. It worked!

Glancing all around, I saw Cade also sprawled out on the floor. He'd faired a bit worse than I did. It looked like he'd hit his head on the table, and there was a red mark just above his right eye. He blinked at me, then smiled.

"You did it, Nic. You got us home."

A happy bleep came from the corner, and I sat up to find Tinker upside down, propped up against one of the shelves.

"Are we sure it's the right timeline?"

Sitting up too, Cade inspected the room. "I'm sure. These are the books we were reading when we left. And that's your backpack on that chair." He pointed to the table behind us.

I swiveled around to get a better view, and yes, he was right. My backpack sat in the chair I'd set it in before all of this craziness happened. Even the wrapper from the granola bar I'd eaten was there. Something told me that we'd come back to almost the exact moment we'd initially left. That no time had passed here, while we'd spent a couple of days jumping from timeline to timeline.

With a grunt, I grabbed onto the table beside me and hauled myself to my feet. My knee smarted a bit, so I didn't put much weight on it. Looking around at the mess we'd made, I bent down to pick up the big book I'd landed on, which was splayed open on a certain section. When I went to set it on the table, my gaze swept over the page, and stopped.

"Holy shit. Look at this, Cade."

He came over and looked down to where I pointed

on the page. The section of the book was on the God Dionysus in particular. There was even an illustration included.

The picture showed a baby swaddled in white cloth. Holding the baby was a dome shaped metal creature, and with it were two people—a young woman with long black hair in a ponytail, wearing blue pants and a white shirt, and a young man with shaggy black hair and vivid blue eyes. He wore what looked like a jump-suit. Under the illustration it read:

"As an infant, Dionysus was delivered to the maenads by three strangers. The maenads called them The Travelers."

"It's us!" My head started to swim, so I pulled out the closest chair and sat down in it before I fainted.

"That's… that's crazy."

"How is that possible?"

Cade rubbed his mouth. "Well, technically that's how it happened. We found Dionysus and brought him to the maenads. That is what happened in the past."

I shook my head. "I have a headache."

"This is why I kept insisting we didn't interfere with the events that unfolded. Or we would alter history. Just like we did here." He gestured to the illustration. "Luckily, it didn't alter the course of history. It was supposed to happen like this." His eyes closed and he sighed. "I have a headache too."

"Now what do we do?"

"Get some sleep. And in the morning, we'll try and put the pieces together."

"Are you sure it's safe for me to sleep? What if I accidentally send my arse somewhere?"

A few chuckles escaped him. "I'm pretty sure you'll be fine."

"Pretty sure, isn't one hundred percent sure."

"You will be okay, Nic."

I swallowed, unsure if I should ask for what I really wanted right now. "Will you stay with me? At least until I fall asleep?"

Warmth gleamed in his eyes, and he nodded. "Yeah."

After we did a quick pick up of all the books on the floor—because we didn't want to incite Athena's wrath by leaving a huge mess in her library—Cade walked me to my room. Luckily, we didn't run into anyone, so we didn't have to explain why we were wearing blood stained, dirty togas, and looked like we'd just walked out of a war zone, which technically we kind of had.

"I need a shower," I declared once we were inside my room. Without waiting for his answer, I went into the bathroom and shut the door.

I quickly shed the robe—I was definitely going to burn it later—then stepped into the stall. Turning on the hot water, I let it sluice over my skin, hoping it would wash away the dirt, the confusion, and the pain from the last two days.

My eyes fell closed, and I raised my face to the water. It felt good as the hot, hard spray lashed against my skin. I ran my hands over my hair, then twisted it into a ringlet over my shoulder. I was too tired to wash it right now.

As I opened my eyes, intending to turn off the faucet and step out of the shower stall, I saw Cade through the clear curtain. He stood in the bathroom, watching me. The look on his face told me all I needed to know. For a moment, I thought about covering myself, but I was beyond caring about being exposed and vulnerable. Instead, I opened the stall door.

"Do you want to come in?"

He nodded. "Yes."

CHAPTER FOURTEEN

NICOLE

*A*t first, I was shocked by Cade's bold appearance in the bathroom. I was also too overwhelmed with emotion to even try and work that out in my head. It didn't matter, all that mattered was that he was here, reaching out to me in the most raw and real way possible.

I watched as he slowly stripped off his robe. There was no shame in how he stood naked before me. So, I took him in, every glorious inch of him. His body was lean but muscular. Like an Olympic swimmer with broad shoulders, trim waist, and smooth, silky looking skin.

Once he stepped into the stall, I moved back, into the corner while he drew the curtain closed. My body was shaking. I was so nervous. It wasn't like I hadn't had sex before. I had, a few times, but this was… more. This was everything, and I didn't want to ruin it by doing something stupid, going too fast, or too slow.

Cade's gaze became penetrating but respectful. He didn't devour me with it, just kept staring into my eyes. Slowly, he reached a hand out and cupped the back of my neck, then pulled me too him, wrapping his arms around me.

"Is this okay?"

"Yes." My voice quivered with repressed need.

Our bodies pressed against each other. His chest was hard, his skin smooth like I thought, and I felt his racing heart against my skin. It matched mine, slamming hard against my ribcage. As the hot spray of water washed over him, I drew my hands up and down his back.

He was breathing hard, as was I. His breath puffed along the side of my neck while he gently pressed his lips just below my ear. I gasped and my body jolted, a spear of heat shooting down my spine and settling in between my thighs.

"Did I hurt you?"

"Gods no. You're doing everything right."

Curious hands splayed wide across my back, finger-tips brushing along the sensitive skin of my lower spine. He urged me even closer, and the hard length of his erection pressed against my hip bone. It was a bit uncomfortable, but I didn't mind. It felt powerful to know he desired me so much.

His lips nibbled their way up along my jaw, until he finally, breathlessly, covered my mouth with his.

We kissed, and I lost myself to it, and to him. I'd dreamt of this moment. I didn't realize how much I wanted him until now, my body pressed against his, my lips on his, my tongue sweeping over his in his mouth. I was pretty sure I wanted him the second I laid my eyes on him at the garden. I understood now that although I'd lost my memories of him from before, my body still reacted as if we'd never been apart.

Lips still locked, Cade moved me until my back was set against the shower wall. A hand brushed around my hip, feathering over my belly, and I sucked in a breath as his fingers lowered, sliding in between the juncture of my thighs.

A gasp left me when his fingertips touched my sensitive nerves, then buried deep inside me. Wanting more, I lifted my leg, setting my heel against the wall to give him full access to me.

The muscles in my thighs and belly quivered as he

stimulated me. I threw my head back as a liquid ball of heat swelled deep inside me, swirling like a tornado. I suspected it wouldn't take much for me to orgasm. A few well-placed strokes of his fingers and I'd be off, but I didn't want to come without having him inside me first.

Feeling bold, I dropped a hand between us, and wrapped my fingers around his erection. He hissed between his teeth as I stroked his full length. Boosted by his reaction to me, I took him and guided him to my sex.

One of Cade's hands curled around my waist, the other anchoring him against the wall as he met my gaze. His jaw clenched with restraint. "You're so beautiful, Nicole."

I wanted to tell him that I'd fallen in love with him, but I didn't want to scare him away. Instead, I licked my lips. "So are you."

His fingers dug into my flesh, as he thrust his hips forward, and slid inside me. Slapping my hand onto his shoulder to hang on, I cried out as he filled me completely.

He immediately froze. "Am I hurting you?"

"Fuck, no," I panted. "Keep going or I'll kill you."

A few chuckles left him, but he started to move inside me again. Closing his eyes, Cade grit his teeth with each thrust of his hips. His hand slid around my waist and gripped my ass as he picked up the pace, finding a rhythm that nearly made me cry with pleasure.

Before, when I'd had sex, it always felt good. But this… this was beyond words. The sensations surging through me were indescribable. Explosive heat built deep inside my body, until it wouldn't take much more before I erupted over him.

I wrapped a hand around his neck and pulled his mouth close to mine. My lips pressed against his and I kissed him, hard, as my orgasm suddenly slammed into me.

"Oh, good Gods!"

Cade fell forward, burying his face into my neck and his teeth scraping against my skin, then thrusted harder between my legs. Shaky breaths passed his lips as he too found release.

CHAPTER FIFTEEN

CADE

I could barely take in any air as my heart thundered in my chest. My head rested against Nicole's, while I tried to find the energy to finally move. Her body was still vibrating from her orgasm, so I wrapped my arm around her waist, shifted my hips and slid out of her. She brought down her leg slowly, then sagged against the shower wall with a long, drawn-out sigh.

"You okay?" I asked, which was the lamest thing to say ever after great sex.

"Yup."

"Um, that's good." I took a step back, unsure of

what to do now. Did she want me to hug her, or kiss her? Or to just get the hell out of there? I couldn't tell. Instead, I turned to face the spray of the water and washed off my body.

Stepping out of the shower, I grabbed one of the towels and wrapped it around my waist, then grabbed the other one for Nicole as she too got out. She took it without looking at me and wound it around her body. I hated that everything felt so awkward now.

After drying off, we dressed in our regular clothes that I'd brought back to her room, then came out of the bathroom. Nicole sat on the bed and stretched her arms.

Unsure of what she wanted me to do, I leaned against the wall. "Are you hungry?"

She shook her head, yawning. "I'm tired." She laid down on the bed, tucking the pillow under her head.

"Okay, I'll, ah, go, and—"

"Lay down with me." Nicole held out her hand toward me.

Releasing the nervous breath I was holding, I took her hand and settled beside her on the mattress. She curled into my chest, and I wrapped my arm around her waist. Relieved that she wasn't angry at me, or full of regret, I kissed the top of her head, while she relaxed against me, yawning again.

It didn't take long before she fell asleep. One big jerk of her body, and then she was out. I should've felt tired, we'd been through so much over the past couple of days, and the sex we'd just had had been vigorous and intense, but I was wide awake.

The guilt of what had just happened between us was starting to grip me. All I could think about right now was Iris. Not that we were a couple anymore, because we weren't, we were just friends—although she'd made that hard in the past couple of years. Still, I just kept picturing her in the infirmary cot, wrapped up with bandages on her face, arm, and hands, healing from the burns she'd suffered. Burns that Nicole had given her.

Quietly and gently, I slid out from under Nicole's body, settling her in and tucking the blanket up to her chin. Thankfully, she didn't flinch or make any indication that she noticed my absence. Before turning away, I looked down at her for a moment. She looked so peaceful that I really hoped bad dreams didn't plague her sleep, and she actually got some much-needed rest.

When I opened the door to leave her room, Tinker was there in the corridor, waiting. He perked up when he saw me.

"Have you been here the whole time?" I asked,

suddenly feeling self-conscious about having sex in the shower. We'd given him superior hearing.

"Yes."

"Why?"

"I do not have anywhere else to go. I do not like the other serving robots. They are rude and not very good conversationalists."

I chuckled and patted him on the head. "Fair enough. You can come with me."

"Where are we going? To your room, to sleep?"

"No, I need to go for a walk, if that's all right."

"You have much to think about."

I nodded. "That's true." I knew he likely meant about all the things we'd seen and learned during our time jumps, but it was thoughts about Nicole and Iris that were bothering me. I had a lot of emotions to figure out and get a handle on now.

"Shall we stroll through the maze? It is a pleasant evening out."

"Sure." I knew that Tinker liked going through the maze. Not only did he get to use his outdoor, all terrain wheels, but he liked looking at the stone statues scattered there.

Once, he told me he liked to think about the lives those statues might have lived at one time. I wasn't sure if he was just using his imagination, or if he believed the rumors that all the stone statues were once people who wronged Medusa.

The light of the full moon guided our way through the maze. I'd always thought it was pretty there, but I never felt at home as much as I did in the other garden, the one where Nicole and I had wanted to erect the stone sun dial. It was good to get another perspective. Iris loved the maze, so I had spent a lot of time here with her.

Once at the center, I lit the cauldrons that stood on either side of the gazebo with a flick of my fingers, and sat down inside it, on one of the wooden benches. Tinker occupied himself by tracking the flight of a moth and making notes. I liked that I'd installed learning capabilities in him, but sometimes it was like dealing with a toddler who had a multitude of interests and questions.

As I sat there, I got a whiff of Nicole's hair scent in the light breeze. Her smell was all over me and it was a punch to the gut. I nearly groaned, thinking about her in the shower. How she looked and reacted as I touched her on various parts of her amazing body. How good she felt in my hands, the silkiness of her skin, the heat between her legs. I almost got hard again, picturing her surrendering to me, to us.

"Argh." I leaned forward, putting my head in my hands. Why did it have to be so difficult loving her?

And I was sure that I *did* love her.

I shouldn't have, though. She'd hurt Iris, a girl I had tried hard to love. It had been three years, I knew that, and people changed for sure. Nicole didn't even remember it; she didn't remember who she'd been back then. She was definitely a different person now. Some things were the same, certainly, but a lot had changed.

Did that mean that what I was feeling for her was right?

Iris still suffered. It wasn't fair to her. It would absolutely destroy her if she ever found out about me and Nicole.

I had to keep it a secret, and it couldn't continue. However much it would hurt Nicole and me, I had to keep my distance. It was the right and moral thing to do. Nicole would understand.

CHAPTER SIXTEEN

NICOLE

*W*hen I woke up the next morning, after what I was sure was at least ten hours of deep sleep, I stared up at the ceiling fan and wondered how I was going to face Cade.

It wasn't that I regretted our sexual tryst, I didn't at all, I'd been hoping for it, but I had a suspicion that he was going to regret it because of his loyalty to Iris. Despite him admitting that they weren't together, I knew he still harbored feelings for her and a sense of duty. So, sleeping with the villain who had permanently disfigured her would be in serious contradiction with those parameters.

It made me feel like shit, too. So, there was that. We could be emo pals together.

With a heavy sigh, I rolled out bed and changed my clothes. My stomach growled, obviously I needed some food as well. When I opened the door to my room, I expected to see Tinker waiting for me in the hall, but the corridor was empty of one cute little robot. He must've been with Cade.

However, I did run into the red-headed psychic, or whatever she was, Cassandra. It looked like she'd been waiting for me.

"Good morning," I said to her.

"It's good to see you are back."

My eyes narrowed at her. "Back from where?"

"All over."

I nodded. "Did you have a vision about me?" I whispered.

"Several actually."

"Well, you can tell me all about it as we walk to the dining hall. I have to put some food in my gob before I go absolutely mental."

It wasn't very busy when we walked into the hall. Only a smattering of people sat at the tables, eating. Most were just sitting around, chatting, like the table that Lucian and his friends occupied. I assumed most of the "students" were in class or training.

Cassandra stood with me in the food line as I piled on as much food as I could carry. Time traveling was hungry business. Silently, I wondered if jumping from timeline to timeline used a lot of caloric output. It must've, considering I felt almost hollow inside—as though I hadn't eaten in over a week.

Once I had my food, I carried the tray to a table in the corner. I didn't feel like making small talk to a bunch of people who didn't seem all that pleased to have met me. Lucian, et al. They were nice enough, but I could tell they didn't want me to try to integrate myself into their close-knit group.

Truth be told, I didn't blame them. I mean, Melany Richmond had some epically wicked shoes to fill, and I was definitely not up to par to fill them. Besides that, I didn't really want to.

The moment I sat, I started shoveling food into my mouth as fast as I could while Cassandra just stared at my profile.

For a second, I stopped from chewing and looked at her. "Are you going to tell me what you saw?"

"I saw you walking through a blinding white ray of light."

I frowned. "And that's it?"

"You had a clock for a face."

"Interesting." I went back to my food.

"I know you can move through time."

I froze mid-chew.

"You went to the Gods' War, then the battle with Oceanus—I saw Melany there too—and some battle between Zeus and a king."

"Have you told anyone?"

She shook her head.

"Not even your golden boyfriend?"

"No, not even him."

"Good. And I'd appreciate that you don't say anything to anyone. I don't want anyone to know that I have that ability. Although, I'm not completely sold that I have it alone."

"Why?"

Dropping my fork, I turned on the bench to really look at her. "Because I don't want the Gods to know. I don't want them to be able to use my power for their gain. They already use us enough, don't you think?"

After observing me for a long moment, she slowly nodded. "I won't say anything. And I agree with you, by the way."

That surprised me. I thought everyone at the academy toed the line to some extent. Maybe I was wrong. I hoped I was wrong.

"Thanks."

She gave me a smile that I sensed was a rare thing.

Cassandra didn't seem like a girl who smiled a lot. When her gaze went over my shoulder, her cheeks flushed. I swiveled to see what or who she was looking at, and spotted Cade making his way across the dining hall toward me.

My gaze returned to her. "Please tell me you didn't also see…"

Cassandra didn't answer, she just got up, and quickly walked back to Lucian at their table.

Cade sat down next to me. "Morning. Did you sleep well?"

"I did sleep good, thanks. No dreams." I picked up a couple pieces of bacon and shoved them into my mouth. If I was eating, I didn't have to be talking. "Where's Tink?"

"He's charging up in my room."

His discomfort was palpable, but I didn't comment on it. Instead, I slid my tray toward him. Maybe he could eat his feelings too, then we wouldn't have to talk about what had happened between us. It could just stay in the past, like everything else.

He chose a slice of pizza from my tray and took a bite. "So, we should probably go talk to Prometheus about what we learned."

I nodded. "Okay, but I'd prefer if we don't mention the time traveling part of it."

"Then how did we find all of this out?"

"Good old fashioned book learning." I grabbed a couple of chips, dunked them in some mayo and then ketchup. "We were in the Hall of Learning all night, right?"

Cade studied me for a moment. "You don't want them to know you can manipulate time?"

"No, I bloody well don't. It's bad enough what they already force us to do, I don't want them to be able to make me jump through time and take them with me too. I mean, could you imagine what could happen? What they would be able to do?"

He didn't say anything for a long time, then nodded. "Okay, we won't say anything about our time jumps."

"Good." I grabbed some more chips. "We should probably make sure Tinker doesn't spill the beans either. Can we reprogram him or something?"

"He won't if we tell him not to. He has instructions to do what we ask."

"Okay."

After another couple of awkward moments, Cade cleared his throat, and I really hoped he wasn't going to say or ask what I thought he was going to ask.

"Should we talk about—"

"Nope. We don't need to."

"Nic…"

"What? I think having a conversation is only going to ruin everything."

He tried to grab my hand, but I pulled away. Before we could further fuck up what had been a beautiful time between us by talking, Lucian joined us at the table. He sat down on the bench across from us.

"I think I've found someone who could give us some information about Pegasus," he informed with no preamble. I liked that about him. Cut to the chase without any banal small talk.

"Who?" Cade asked.

"Pan."

Cade let out a low groan.

"Who's Pan?" I inquired, suddenly very curious.

"Not a guy we want to get to know," Cade explained. "How do you know where he is? I heard he's impossible to find, let alone talk to. He's famously reclusive."

"Someone supplied me with the information. A person who owed me—well, owed Melany a favor."

The change in his face when he talked about her was heartbreaking. There was obviously eternal love there. I almost wanted to give him a hug, but I suspected he'd knock me out if I tried.

My attention went to Cade. "I'm up for it, if you are. This Pan sounds like a delightful distraction."

"I got one condition," Lucian added.

"What?" Cade countered.

"That we get to come with you. We're all kind of bored right now."

"No…"

"Absolutely!" I exclaimed, and Cade frowned at me.

"It's not a good idea."

"It's a great idea. I take it this Pan might be trouble-some?" I addressed Lucian.

"Most likely. He doesn't take well to strangers in his woods."

"You see? The more the merrier then." Snatching a slice of pizza from my tray, I stood. "Let's get going. Time's a-wastin'."

Cade gave me a troubled look. I guessed he didn't like my little inside joke.

LUCIAN INSISTED we should arm ourselves before heading to the woods on the far side of the lake. I didn't argue, because I didn't know what to expect with Pan.

I stuck a dagger into my belt after Jasmine insisted I did, but I figured my fire power was sufficient. Cade grabbed a Bo staff, and when he twirled it around expertly, my heart did a little pitter-patter. Who knew he had combat skills? I guessed I would know that if I could remember my past time at the academy.

Once we were fully outfitted, like a band of mercenaries, we all flew to the lake—well, I didn't fly, Cade had to carry me again. On the edge of the shore, Cade and Lucian argued about who was in charge and who was going to lead us into the woods. I just stood back and watched the entertaining show with Jasmine, Mia, Georgina, Ren and Cassandra.

I considered making small talk with the others, but honestly, they all kind of intimidated me. So, I did what I did best, and made a joke.

"Hey, you two. Do you want a ruler?"

Halting their argument, they both frowned at me, but Cade knew better than to answer. Lucian hadn't learned that lesson yet.

"What for?" he asked.

"So, you can measure your…" I pointed to their crotches. "And see who the big man is."

Everyone beside me snickered at that. Jasmine laughed out loud rather joyously, which made me grin.

She smacked me on the shoulder. "You are funny."

Cade marched over to me. "You're not that funny."

"Yeah, I am."

Lucian took a stance in front of the group. "We go in single file. Hecate told me that there may be snares and tripwires around the perimeter of his location."

I held up my hand. "I'm sorry, what now? I didn't realize we were going into a war zone."

Cade threw me a knowing look, the one that said, 'I told you so.'

Jasmine's hand smacked my shoulder again. "I got you. You can go after me."

"Thank you, Jasmine. I feel better already." I gave her what I hoped was a winning smile, and it didn't come off as condescending. I really didn't want to piss her off too. She looked like she could fold me in half.

Actually, they all did.

Mia was a bit skinnier, but the look she was giving me told me that it didn't matter how slim she was, she'd rip me apart as well. Part of me wondered if it was because Jasmine was paying me some attention and she was jealous.

Lucian went first into the woods. Then Cassandra, Georgina, Ren, Mia, Jasmine, me, and Cade at the end. The way the boys were positioned, the whole thing almost felt sexist. Yet, I didn't say anything. They were going to have my back, I assumed, so I wasn't going to rock the boat. Not when I was the most likely to drown if we capsized.

We hadn't gone more than ten feet, before Lucian gave the signal to stop moving. "There's a tripwire here." He pointed to it, and then to what would happen if we tripped it.

There was a very large tree branch with spikes on it positioned on a tree a few feet away. I imagined it would snap forward and impale the poor sucker who hadn't seen the wire across the path.

This was turning into the scariest situation I'd ever been in, and that was saying something, considering Cade and I had just been through two wars with the Gods.

CHAPTER SEVENTEEN

NICOLE

After Lucian carefully cut the wire, we continued walking on the narrow dirt path deeper into the dark woods. We came across two other traps, another tripwire and a snare that appeared to be for catching rabbits, us being the rabbits.

Once Lucian dismantled the last one, the woods seemed to go incredibly quiet. Lively bird songs surrounded us before, crickets, and the scurry of rodents on the forest floor. Now, however, there was nothing. Not even the wind blew through the leaves of the giant oak and willow trees.

I leaned into Cade. "I'm going to go out on a limb and predict that this is not a good thing," I murmured.

"Be ready," Lucian barked.

After another few tense moments, Georgina stepped off the path and approached one of the large willow trees. Her hand lifted toward it. "I can see you. We haven't come to hurt you. We just want to speak with Pan."

Just like that, it suddenly looked like the entire forest was moving. A sea of green surging toward us.

From among the trees, stepped out diminutive women with green and brown skin, and hair made of leaves. They were all topless, one of the reasons I knew they were women, but wore skirts made of leaves and grass. Each one of them, and there had to be at least twenty, carried a sharpened spear.

It was like déjà vu for Cade and I, being greeted by the maenads in the woods three thousand years ago.

As one, they opened their tiny mouths, and a series of loud and high-pitched chirps erupted. It was like a thousand birds chirping all at the same time, each hitting varying high notes. My head instantly hurt, and I put my hands over my ears to try and muffle the piercing noise. It was useless, I could still hear it, and it sent a zip of pain through my skull.

A few minutes later, we were all down on our knees

on the soil, hands on our ears trying not to go insane, and hoping our eardrums didn't burst. Then it all stopped, dead still, and there was lovely blissful silence. Except, there was also a ringing in my ears. When we all stood, I assumed everyone else was experiencing it too, judging by the pained looks on their faces.

Another figure stepped out of the foliage. He stood maybe five feet tall, with little horns on top of his head that peered out from under long, curly dark hair. His bottom half was that of a goat, exhibiting cloven hooves and tail, while his top half was that of a man.

He also had a moustache and a long beard that matched his hairy, muscular chest and arms. The most surprising thing about him though, was that he was strangely attractive. Or maybe that was just me being weird and pervy.

"I could make them chirp all day long if I so wanted. It would rupture your ear drums for sure, and maybe even worse. Once, I saw one guy's eyes actually burst out of his skull. It was rather gross."

"We'd prefer if that didn't happen," Lucian replied.

"What do you want? Why are you trespassing in my woods?"

Cade stepped forward. "We've come for information."

"What kind of information?"

Lucian whipped around, shooting eye daggers towards Cade.

"About the Pegasus," Cade continued, not fazed by Lucian, and I loved that. "Since Artemis is no longer with us, we heard that you are very knowledgeable and that she trusted you with her knowledge."

Cade was smart, trying to appeal to the guy's ego. Something told me that despite his small stature, Pan had an enormous sense of himself.

"What have you brought me for this knowledge?"

Oh shit. Did we even think about that? I knew I hadn't.

Once more, Cade had thought ahead. Unzipping the backpack he carried, he pulled out a pair of funky looking metal goggles and lifted them. "These glasses, from Hephaistos. You will be able to see for miles."

That seemed to please Pan.

Cade also pulled out a leather water bag. "Wine, from Dionysus."

The little Faun looked even more pleased about that. "What else?" he asked excitedly.

Cade's face fell. He'd obviously thought these two gifts would be enough for Pan. The rest of our group kind of looked at each other, but I pulled out the dagger from my belt.

"How about this cool dagger?" I held it up to him. "It's got sparkly gems on the hilt."

Pan's eyes narrowed with interest, telling me he was really close to accepting our bargain. On a whim, I snatched Jasmine's bow off her back and showed to him too. "And this awesome bow."

A growl escaped Jasmine's throat, but I didn't make eye contact with her. It was best that way.

"Deal," Pan declared. "Come to my village and we will eat, and drink, and…" His gaze raked over me hungrily. "…make merry."

Yikes. Guys had flirted with me before, but his level of flirtation was intense. Somehow, I actually felt his gaze on my skin. A shiver rushed down my back—a not entirely unpleasant shiver to my surprise.

As we followed him to his village, Jasmine grabbed my arm and pulled me close. "I should hurt you for giving away my favorite bow."

"But you won't, because I'm so funny and like-able?" I grinned, blinking up at her innocently.

Slowly nodding, she let go of my arm. "Exactly. Plus, I can get another bow."

Thank the Gods! I sighed with relief. The last thing I needed was to be beat up by one of my allies.

"Thanks for the quick thinking," Cade offered, coming over to my side.

"Hey, you're the one who was smart enough to bring gifts. I was just going with your flow, mate." I winked at him. "But I don't think Jasmine is too happy with me though. And I'm not sure I'm doing this *make new friends* thing correctly."

He laughed, and I loved hearing the sound.

"We make a good team," he concluded.

A small smile curved my lips. "Yeah, we do."

PAN'S VILLAGE consisted of several sleeping huts—a large, round hut built on top of a wooden base, and a few houses built into mounds of dirt. There were fruit trees surrounding the area, as well as a narrow stream that meandered on the edge of the huts.

The village was formed by several, pretty little wood nymphs and Pan. No wonder he was so reclusive. He had everything a goat man could want. Plenty of food, water, and... companionship. Also, I had a sense that he didn't want to share.

"Come." Pan went into the large, round hut, and we followed.

Surprise greeted us inside the hut. Honestly, I expected some wooden benches to sit on, or grassy cushions, but it looked like a Greek God's opulent oasis, dedicated to decadence and overindulgence.

At the back of the hut was a raised dais, and on that dais, sat an elegant golden lounger—plumped with silk pillows of all colors. Actually, almost every square inch of the wooden floor was covered with more colorful silk pillows and fur blankets. A table piled high with fruit, nuts, breads, and cooked wild game like partridges and duck, was placed in the middle of the space. There were also plenty of jugs of wine.

"Sit." He pointed to the pillows on the floor, as he walked up the few steps on the dais, and lounged on his sofa. One of the wood nymphs instantly scurried toward him, holding a bunch of grapes to feed him one grape at a time.

He seemed literally pulled out of one of those old paintings in museums, about the lasciviousness of the Greek Gods.

The moment we sat down, all in a nervous cluster, several of the nymphs rushed over and started to serve us food and wine. I thought it would be rude to refuse, so I gladly took a cup of wine and some bread. Cade also eagerly indulged, although the others were a bit more cautious.

It showed that they'd never traveled back three thousand years to party with a group of maenads. Smiling to myself about that, I took a big gulp of wine. It was really tasty and went straight to my head.

"You."

My head snapped up to see Pan pointing at me. "Um, me?"

"Yes. You seem like a woman who knows how to play the game. Why don't you come up here, and sit with me?"

I glanced over at Cade for help, making a 'do I?' face.

He shrugged.

Finally, I decided there was no harm in indulging Pan. So, I got up, climbed up onto the dais and sat beside him on his magnificent lounger. The nymph at his side offered to feed me some grapes too.

Why the hell not? I thought, and opened my mouth so she could place a single plump, purple globe onto my tongue. It was a taste explosion in my mouth.

"So, what do you want to know about the Pegasus?"

"Basically, everything you know about its nature and its powers," Cade answered for the group.

Ignoring my friend, Pan turned to me. "Why don't you shuffle a little closer, and I'll whisper all my secrets into your ear."

My face flushed, and I actually giggled. Was it hot in here? Because it sure felt hot. Sweat rolled down my back. "Um, you could just say it out loud, for the whole group."

"I like you. You amuse me." He grinned at me, and my throat went dry. Holy hotness! What was going on here?

The Faun gulped a big cup of wine, held it out to be filled again by the nymph, and then addressed Cade. "There are two tales about how the Pegasus came to be. In the first, he was made from sea foam and blood in the great ocean. The second says he was birthed from the freshwater spring on Mount Helicon, and tended to by the twelve muse sisters." He drank more wine. "All I can say to that is, I wish I was tended to by the muse sisters. They are very attractive."

He wiggled his bushy eyebrows at me, and I giggled again. Either the wine was making me giddy, or he was. Perhaps it was a combination, but I couldn't be the only one being affected by it, was I?

Glancing over at the others, I saw Cassandra with her head on Lucian's shoulder; he was happily playing with her hair. Jasmine and Mia were actually snogging. Ren was giving Georgina a foot rub while she lounged on the pillows, wine in one hand, and berries in the other. Cade, however, was staring at me, his gaze laser focused, and I could almost hear his thoughts. They were pretty racy.

He shook his head though, trying to keep it clear. It was obvious he was the only one that had any type of will power over whatever spell was being cast inside the hut.

"What else?" he asked. "What kind of powers does the Pegasus have?"

"Well, the myth about the only person who can ride Pegasus has to be pure of heart is absolute bullshit. I mean, all the Gods could ride him, and we all know there is nothing pure about the Gods. Except, maybe for Artemis. She was truly decent and chaste. I could never tempt her. She had her flaws, certainly, but that wasn't one of them."

"I rode Pegasus," Lucian shouted.

Pan chuckled and waved a hand toward him. "So, there you go. That myth is most definitely busted."

That made everyone in the hut laugh. Including Lucian.

"Obviously, the beast can fly. He can find water anywhere. If you were in the desert and thirsty, he could paw at the sand and find you a spring. It's amazing actually. He's the only creature that can enter Olympus. And he could probably kill you with a flap of his wings. His feathers are almost like steel."

Pan turned to me again, a hand patting my leg.

"And that's that. Nothing else I can tell you,

because there is nothing else to tell." He then stretched out his legs, setting his furry feet and hooves on my lap. "Now, let's have a party, shall we? I find you all so very attractive. Especially you, funny girl."

"I could party." With a smile, I ran my fingers over his hooves. It was really weird, but I was kind of digging it right now.

CHAPTER EIGHTEEN

NICOLE

I didn't know what time it was when we all staggered out of Pan's hut, and into the twilight. Judging by how low the sun was in the sky, I'd say it was eight or nine o'clock at night, which meant we had been inside his hut for no less than eight hours.

What had transpired inside was a bit of a blur to me. I could picture bits and pieces, snippets of more wine and food, and dancing?

I glanced at Cade as he scratched his head and frowned. It appeared he was having just as much difficulty putting the pieces together as I was. Lucian looked about the same, so did the others. Exchanging a quick glance with Jasmine, my cheeks flushed. Maybe the two of us had shared a kiss or two. Mia's eye daggers in the back of my head confirmed that.

"Okay, what just happened in there?" I asked after a few more disoriented minutes. Someone had to while we all just shuffled around in front of the hut.

Cade smacked his lips. "I'm not too sure. One thing I do know though, is that I drank way too much wine. Again."

"I did too," Georgina confirmed, rubbing her head. "I have the worst headache."

In that moment, Pan strutted out of the hut, his hooves clacking on the wooden platform like a woman's high heels on floor tile. "Thank you so much for visiting, gang. You were all sublime. Especially you, Nicole." He blew me a kiss.

My stomach flipped, and I rubbed it. I really hoped what he was implying didn't actually occur. I was an open-minded person, and believed that love was love no matter what—it wasn't anyone's business what went on in people's bedrooms—but... this...

I leaned toward Cade. "Um, did I..."

"Pretty sure there was just a lot of drinking and dancing. And maybe a few shared kisses... but other than that, no. You definitely did not. I wouldn't have let that happen."

Relief coursed through me warm and sweet. "Okay. As long as you are sure."

"I'm sure."

"I do have an image of kissing him though."

Cringing, Cade rubbed his mouth. "I'm pretty sure I did too."

A bubble of laughter came out of me, I couldn't help it. The horrified look on Cade's face was comical. I wanted to tell him that it didn't mean anything, but I kind of wanted him to squirm a bit about it first. It was all a bit of harmless fun anyway.

Waving Pan goodbye, I got back on the path to get the hell out of there. Everyone pretty much hurried up behind me. We weren't worried about trip wires or traps anymore; we'd already endured the freakiest ambush ever.

When we landed back at the academy, everyone scattered after some awkward goodbyes. Lucian was probably regretting asking us to come along on our little adventure into *weirdsville*. Cade and I went inside to find Prometheus and confer with him about everything we'd learned over the past few days.

Once Cade flew us up to the highest floor in the

hall, Prometheus's office, we found the big man sitting at his desk, reading something. An honest smile lit up his face when he saw us, however, I had a feeling he knew we were coming. My gaze searched the room to see if the eyeless prophet was lurking about in the shadows, ready to jump out at me, but found nothing.

He gestured to the chairs by his desk. "Please, sit."

"We have a lot of information to discuss with you," Cade admitted.

"Excellent. I'm sure together we will be able to figure out who this Corpse King is and what he wants."

I plopped down in one of the chairs, setting my foot up on my other knee. "We already figured out who the Corpse King is."

His eyebrows arched. "Really? Who is he?"

"King Lycaon," Cade offered.

"Interesting." Prometheus steepled his fingers together and pressed them to his mouth. "What does he want with the Pegasus?"

"Not quite sure yet," I confessed, "but he definitely wants revenge."

"Against who?"

"Zeus, for cursing his sons to turn into wolves, and against Aphrodite and Ares for helping him slaughter them in a horrible, disgusting way." It was hard to keep the contempt out of my voice.

"That does sound horrible, but Zeus, Aphrodite, and Ares are all dead. How could he get revenge on them?"

He had a good point. It was something we hadn't thought of clearly. I glanced at Cade; he had the same confused furrow to his brow.

"And why steal the Pegasus? How does that get him revenge?"

Becoming silent, I went over all that Pan told us about Pegasus. I didn't think it had anything to do with finding water or his steel wings. Yet, it was definitely about flying, or else he would've stolen a few of the fire horses—they were faster and stronger than the Pegasus. And where could he fly to, that no other beast could go?

"He needs the Pegasus to get into Olympus," I blurted. "He's the only beast that can enter the mountain."

Prometheus nodded. "That does seem to track. But why Olympus? What is there for him? What does he need to get his revenge on Zeus when he's already gone?"

Cade and I both looked at each other, the answer flashing in our minds. "Time."

The memory of something Aphrodite had said when we saw them in France returned to me… "*Yes, well, neither of us can control time."*

"He wants to go back in time," I informed.

"How? And what does Olympus have to do with this?"

I didn't know the answer, but it was there somewhere. It had to be. It was all starting to make sense.

Considering it, Cade rubbed at his forehead, until his eyes lit up with a clue. "The Hours. They live in Olympus."

Prometheus's brow creased deeply, and he dropped his hands on the desk. "Yes, but of what use would they be? They don't have any real power. They can't manipulate time."

"How many of them are there?" I asked.

"Twelve," Cade answered.

Something poked my mind, an image that had bothered me since seeing it. In the vision, when Cassandra and I visited the gray man, Cronus, I saw a giant stone wheel. That same wheel was in an illustration of Cronus in a book, and in both cases, there were twelve pegs on it.

"Only Cronus has that power..." Aphrodite's voice once again echoed in my mind.

"The Corpse King is going to kidnap them. He's going to take the Hours and figure out a way to find

Cronus. The God of Time is the only one that has the power to change things with his wheel of time."

Heaving a heavy sigh, Prometheus sat back in his chair, regarding me thoughtfully. "You're right about time. Cronus is the only one who can change it or move it."

I refrained from telling him that I could manipulate time too. No one needed to know, so it would remain my and Cade's secret. My eyes connected with his, to make sure he wouldn't accidentally, or purposely, out me. Fortunately, he gave me a reassuring smile, and I relaxed a little. Of course, he wouldn't say anything. I was an idiot for thinking otherwise.

"I'm not sure if your kidnapping theory is valid, though. It would take an army for him to take twelve people from Olympus, but we will definitely put the mountain on alert."

How about an army of the dead? I wanted to scream. The Corpse King had an army, and he had the means now to get that army to Olympus and take the Hours. The entire army couldn't fly on one Pegasus, but he could hitch a chariot to the flying horse and bring as many of the dead as he could stuff into the vehicle.

"Let's send the academy's army there. I mean, that's what this is all for, isn't it?" I gestured to his fortress in the sky. "To protect and serve the community at large."

"This is true. That is what the academy was initially built for, but I don't think this warrants an entire army to go to Olympus. We have other matters to take care of. There was a tornado that just wiped out a whole town in the United States. We're going there to help clean up and rebuild. There are wildfires raging in Argentina and Chile that we are fighting. We do more than just war here, Nicole."

"I'll go to Olympus and make sure that it is fortified," Cade offered, and Prometheus nodded in acceptance.

"A better solution. Thank you, Cade. You can leave immediately and check in with me daily."

Cade stood, and I followed. I was about to say something most likely hostile and stupid, when Cade grabbed my hand and tugged me closer to him. He put his arm around my shoulders. "Thank you for seeing us."

"Of course. Keep me in the loop."

After Cade ushered me to the edge of the platform, I wrapped my arms around him, and he flew us down to the first floor. When my feet hit the floor, I broke away from him.

"He's a pompous ass. He's not even listening to what we're telling him."

"It is all conjecture at this point, Nic. We don't know for sure that is what he wants to use Pegasus for."

I gave him a dubious look. "You know we're right. We didn't jump all over time for no reason."

"Look, I'll go to Olympus and make sure the Hours are warned. That's really all we can do right now."

"And what am I supposed to do while you're gone?"

"Get some rest. Train. Get back in fighting shape."

"Both of those things are boring."

That made him chuckle.

"And you don't think I'm in shape?" I flexed my arm. There was the tiniest of a bicep bump.

"I think you are perfect."

He walked me to my room, and we stood there at the closed door awkwardly. Briefly, I thought about inviting him in, but I was pretty sure he'd make up some excuse about how he had to get to Olympus like right now, so I didn't bother. I didn't really want to be rejected right now.

Seeming uncomfortable, he rubbed his arm. "Ah, maybe we should talk about last night."

"Should we? Why?"

"I don't know, so we're on the same page…"

"The page we are on, Cade, is that we had sex. We

were both feeling raw and vulnerable, and we succumbed to years of pent-up attraction for each other. It doesn't need to be any more than that, does it?" I gave him a pointed look. "I mean, it can't be more, can it? Not with our past getting in the way."

Cade's hand lifted to touch me, but he thought better of it, and shoved it into his pants' pocket. "It was more than just sex, and we both know it."

"Okay, so it was great sex."

"You know what I mean."

"Yeah, I do, but it doesn't matter. We both feel too guilty to do anything about it."

He looked at me for a long moment, knowing I was right. I hated being right. For once I wanted so desperately to be wrong, and for Cade would just grab me and throw me up against the wall, then kiss me silly.

"I'll tell Tinker to come stay with you until I'm back. I'll keep in touch and let you know if I hear or see anything."

"Awesome. Sounds just marvelous." I rolled my eyes.

With a resigned nod, he turned and left. His steps suddenly stopped halfway down the corridor, and he marched back to me. Cade grabbed me by my upper arms, and yanked me to him. Without warning, he smashed his mouth to mine, and kissed me until I couldn't breathe. Once he was done, he set me down, and walked away.

I couldn't stop the stupid grin that spread across my face. Maybe we'd get through this together, despite all the bullshit that kept us apart. Time would tell. As it did with just about everything. We knew that better than most.

CHAPTER NINETEEN

CADE

*a*s I walked away from Nicole, I mentally gave myself a slap in the face. What was I thinking kissing her like that? It acted like a promise to something more between us. A promise I wasn't sure I could keep. I was an asshole.

Upon returning to my room, I found Tinker still in the corner—asleep but fully charged. The instant I unplugged him, his eyes flickered open.

"Good morning, Cade."

"Good morning, Tink." It wasn't morning, it was night, but he said that every time he awoke from his charging sleep mode.

I grabbed my backpack and shoved some clothes and other things I might need into it.

"Where are we going?" Tinker asked as he wheeled closer, to see if there was something he could do to help. Grabbing more clothes, he put them in my bag. Clothes I didn't need, so I had to put them back into the drawer and shut it before he did it again.

"I'm going to Olympus on a scouting mission, and you're going to go stay with Nicole."

"What is my mission?"

"To keep her out of trouble."

A few quick bleeps sputtered out of him. "I suspect my mission will be extremely difficult and wrought with danger."

"I suspect that as well," I admitted with a chuckle. "But you just do the best you can." I sat down on the edge of my bed and sighed. "Just be there for her, Tink. She needs a friend."

"And I am her best friend," he added proudly.

"Yes, you are. You're mine too."

He happily blooped, then reached out one of his claw hands and tried to hold mine. I let him, because it was very sweet, I just wouldn't tell anyone about it. Not even Nicole. She'd take the piss, as she used to like to say.

Slinging my bag over my shoulder I left my room.

Once Tinker and I said our goodbyes, he wheeled down the corridor toward Nicole's room while I headed toward the tower. At the top, I unlocked the "door" to the realm of Olympus and walked through it.

As usual, I emerged in the garden. Because it was night and not day, I was greeted by the biggest and fullest moon possible. Moonlight cascaded over the flowers and plants in the garden, and I was struck at how beautiful everything was there, no matter the time or day or the season.

While I walked the path toward the main temple, I spotted movement near the willow trees. A woman in a dark violet robe, violet skin and hair, moved in my direction. Every now and then I would lose sight of her, because she would blend into the darkness around us, but then the shadows would shift again and I could see her approaching. It was a bit unnerving.

"Good evening, Cade. It is most pleasant to see you. We have not crossed paths in many months."

"Good evening, Arctos. Yes, it has been that long. I'm not often in Olympus at this late hour, but I was hoping to find you."

"Well, I am happy to be found." She smiled.

"I don't want to alarm you, but it's quite possible that an evil man we call the Corpse King, might come to Olympus to kidnap you and your sisters."

"Oh, well now, that is quite alarming."

"I thought I should warn you. I want you and the others to be on the lookout for anything out of the ordinary."

"Thank you for the warning, Cade. It is most appreciated. Although we are in the safest possible place in the universe, I will inform my sisters of the potential threat."

"I plan to remain in Olympus to keep an eye on things," I assured, nodding. "I will inform the guards as well, so they can keep an eye on you and your sisters as you take your walks through the garden."

Reaching out, Arctos lightly touched my hand, causing a cold shiver to rush down my spine. Then she turned and continued her nightly walk over the grounds of the mountain.

I watched her leave for a moment, keeping my gaze on the sky for a flash of white, then continued to the temple. First, I needed to stash my bag in the room I used to live in, then I could start the process of informing the guards and other keepers about the Corpse King.

The corridors were fairly empty in the temple as I walked through them, heading to the wing where all the workers in Olympus lived. At one time, I suspected this wing was called the servants quarters, and sometimes I did feel like one here.

I mean, I didn't get paid in any real manner for the work I did. In the end, I understood it was for the greater good, and I wasn't going anywhere, so I didn't require a bank account full of money. I had a room to sleep in, all the food and drink I needed and wanted, entertainment, and a purpose.

When I reached my room, I opened the door and went in without turning on the lights. It wasn't needed, I could move through the room blindfolded. I tossed my bag down near the closest, and went to sit on the bed, when I heard a soft shuffling sound. Flicking my fingers together, a yellow ball of light ignited in my hand, and I waved it toward the bed to see someone moving under the covers.

I pulled the covers and Iris jolted up, trying to yank the covers back over herself. Thankfully, she was wearing a pajamas.

"Cade! What are you doing?"

Marching over to the table, I turned on the lamp. "What are you doing here? This is my room."

"You haven't been in it for months, so I didn't think it was a big deal to sleep here."

"What's wrong with your room? It's bigger and has more comforts. It's an executive suite in fact."

She pulled the blanket up to her nose and inhaled. "I wanted to be close to you. I miss you. I hated the way we left it the last time we saw each other."

Sighing, I went and sat in the chair opposite to the bed. "I'm sorry, Iris. You just really surprised me and I'm a bit on edge."

"Why? What's happened?"

I wasn't sure if I should tell her anything. She was in a fragile state, and I didn't want to unnecessarily upset her. "Nothing to worry about. I'm just here to make sure all the systems are working properly."

Her hand patted the bed beside her. "Come here and I'll give you one of my famous shoulder massages. I remember how much you loved them."

"Iris…"

"No strings attached. Just one friend helping another. We are friends still, aren't we, Cade?"

"Of course we are."

"Then get your butt over here." She patted the bed again.

Without any excuses left to give her that wouldn't hurt her feelings, I went to sit next to her. The guilt of having sex with Nicole was still raw in my gut, so I definitely didn't want to upset her needlessly.

Kneeling on the mattress, Iris positioned herself behind me, so she could access my shoulders. Her hands rested on my neck, beginning to knead and rub my muscles. I did love her massages. She was really good at them, and they always left me feeling relaxed. I was overly tense, so I appreciated the offer.

"Gods, your muscles are tight." She really pressed her thumbs into my trapezoids. "What have you been doing that's so intense and vigorous?"

I hated that I could feel my face flushing. Thankfully, it was still pretty dim in the room, and she wasn't facing me. The last thing I wanted was to have to explain my reaction to her.

"I've been doing some extra training. Keeping my skills sharp."

"Oh, I thought it was because you've been running around with Nicole Walker." Her hands pressed hard into my shoulders, her short nails purposely digging into them.

Shocked, I pulled away from her, and got off the bed, facing her.

"I still have friends in the academy. They keep me up to date on things."

"You're spying on me?" My blood began to boil, but there was also dread coursing through me.

She frowned and sat back on her heels. "No. It's not like that."

"Sounds like that to me, Iris."

"I'm lonely here, Cade. You left me, remember? I like knowing what is going on at the academy, since I can't be there."

Frustration rose, and I scrubbed my face, getting momentously tired by the second. We'd had this conversation before. And before. And before.

"But you *can* be there, Iris. You could come back to the academy to train and be useful again."

Her eyes narrowed into slits. "Are you saying I'm useless?"

I threw up my hands in the air. "No! Gods, that's not what I'm saying. You're putting words in my mouth, as usual."

She'd been doing that lately. Making assumptions about what I was thinking, doing, or saying, just because I didn't always say things quickly enough, or exactly what she wanted to hear. It was exhausting to always be walking on eggshells with her, and one of the reasons I'd left Olympus to go back to the academy.

Pouting, Iris reached a hand toward me. "I don't want to fight. Come here and hug me."

"I don't want to fight either."

Still, I didn't return to the bed. I didn't want to hug her, because I knew what she wanted it to turn into. It was one of her many ploys of keeping us in some sort of relationship. A hug would lead to a kiss, a kiss would lead to some heavy petting, then, most likely, it would lead to sex. She always initiated it, and I was too much of a coward, too riddled with guilt at what had happened to her, to say no and disappoint her.

But I didn't want to go down that path with her anymore.

Her eyes widened as she scowled, her lips pressing into a thin, cold line. "How can you be friends with her, again, after what she did to me?"

Silence was my only answer, because I didn't want to tell her that I wasn't convinced what happened all those years ago, on the obstacle course, had been purposeful. I still believed it had been an accident, and that Nicole was so overwrought with guilt, that she accepted the Gods' decision to wipe her memory and banish her from the academy.

To be tossed out, literally, onto the streets to fend for herself. She wouldn't admit it back then, even when I begged her to tell me the truth. Of course, she couldn't tell me now either, as she didn't have her memories of it, but I believed it. The Nicole I had… loved—I might as well admit it to myself now—didn't have that type of cruelty and hate inside of her.

No one could tell me or prove to me otherwise.

"Because I believe in forgiveness, Iris. I believe in

redemption. I think we all have the capacity to do bad things, but people can, and do, change."

She didn't say anything, just glared at me for the longest time. Finally, she got out of the bed, and left the room, slamming the door shut behind her. I should've gone after her, but I was too tired to, and I had a job to do.

After stowing my bag away, I left the room, and went in search of the temple guards. None could be found in the main pantheon, which was odd. There were usually two or three patrolling the corridors, even at this time of night.

Walking out the main exit to the veranda, I continued searching. There were usually a couple of guards there as well, watching over the entrance and the path to the garden. Yet, the veranda was empty of any sign of them. A ball of dread swelled in my gut. There could've been a logical explanation for it, but something told me it was more than that.

My gaze scanned the foliage and flora for some sign of danger as I rushed down the path to the garden. I went to the willow trees where Arcus usually spent her time when she was convalescing in the garden.

"Arcus?" I called out with urgency.

I didn't get an answer, but I did see a flash of white streak by in the sky. The Corpse King was here.

CHAPTER TWENTY

NICOLE

I knew I should've been sleeping, resting, or maybe even training, but those things were too boring for me right now. Everything in me said I needed to get prepared for what I knew was going to happen.

For the past few days, I'd felt woefully untrained and in need of constant rescue—I wanted to change that. I didn't want to rely on Cade to fly me places, regardless of how good it felt to be pressed that close to him.

Along the way to Hephaistos's forge, I ran into Tinker. Or I should've said, he literally ran into me, blocking me from going down the stone staircase to the underground.

"Where are you going, Nicole?"

"I think you know where I'm going, Tink."

"Cade thought you might want to rest."

"Well, Cade isn't here, and I'm going to do what I want to do. And right now, that's going to the forge and seeing if Hephaistos has finished making my wings." Stepping around the robot, I started down the steps. I glanced over my shoulder at him, as he pouted. He'd even made a little whiny sounds, it was quite pathetic. "Aren't you coming?"

He perked up and switched his regular wheels, so he could come down the stairs without falling. When we reached the bottom, he wheeled through the big open doors beside me, humming a spritely tune. I chuckled.

Upon entering the forge, I heard voices coming from the highest platform. Leaving Tinker on the main level to wheel around at his leisure, I ran up the rickety stone steps to the top, and found Hephaistos there with Dionysus, and Demeter. It looked like they were several drinks into a long night of drinking.

Hephaistos's deep scowl deepened even further when he spotted me, creating large creases in his forehead. "What in the blazes are you doing here?"

"What in the blazes are you guys doing?" Picking up the jug on the stone table they were all leaning on, I sniffed it. It was wine. "Having a wee party?"

Demeter took a puff on the joint hanging between her lips. "I'd forgotten how funny you were."

"Yeah, I'm a joke a minute."

"What are you doing here?" Hephaistos demanded again—with a growl that time.

"I've come to see if you've finished my wings. I need them."

"What for?"

I shrugged. "I don't know. Battle."

"Girl, we're in peace times. There are no battles." He poured himself another full cup and gulped it. It almost sounded like he hated peace times.

"You never know when a battle is on the horizon." My attention shifted to Dionysus. He was leaning on the table, rather precariously, staring at me.

"I remember you from somewhere," he admitted.

"Ah, yeah. I was here three years ago for training."

He frowned, rolling his bottom lip up. "Nope. That's not it."

"I'm sure it will come to you." I grabbed the jug of wine and chugged a bit. "Hmm, this tastes a bit Figgy to me."

Dionysus's eyes went wide, and I had to suppress a

chuckle. Deciding to let him deal with that childhood trauma, I turned back to Hephaistos. "Can I please have my wings?"

"Ugh. You are a giant pain in my ass."

"I know, but I'm fun, right?"

"Debatable," he grumbled, but he did push away from the table and started down the steps to the main floor, where he kept all of his finished pieces.

Dionysus and Demeter didn't follow. They were obviously more interested in their drinks. I, on the other hand, nearly tripped and fell into the canals of molten metal, I was so jazzed.

Hephaistos moved toward his wall of shields and swords, removing a very bulky, folded brass piece. It looked really heavy. "Come here. Turn around."

Happily, I did as he instructed. I was vibrating with excitement.

"Hold out your arms."

Once I did, he slid on two thick leather straps, much like the straps of a backpack, over my shoulders. There was another leather piece that he buckled around my ribs, just above my waist. When he was done, he took a step back, and I felt the full weight of what he'd just strapped onto my back. I nearly fell backwards.

"You're going to have to hunch over, at least until

your back gets strong enough to support the weight of the mechanics."

Bending my knees, I leaned forward a little. It felt a bit easier.

"There are buttons on the underside of each strap. Push them to expand your wings."

Curious, I slid my hands under the straps, but Hephaistos grabbed me and pulled me away from his workstation. "Careful, you'll knock everything off the walls."

Nodding, I moved out from the corner and into an open area of the forge. I took in a deep breath, crazy excited for this moment, then pushed the buttons on the underside of the straps. A whir and a pop echoed in the air, and then an incredible amount of pain captured my shoulder blades, as my wings snapped open on either side of me.

"What the bloody hell!" I reached over my shoulder to try and feel what the hell had just pierced me.

"Don't touch the cables. They are imbedded into your back muscles, so you can fly without having to flap your arms. It simulates the exact thing your peers experience when their wings come out."

The pain began to subside, but there was still a bit of throbbing radiating out down the back of my arms. "You could've warned me."

"Yeah, but what fun would that have been for me?"

I shook my head, but when I looked at each of my metal wings the anger vanished. What I was seeing was way too cool to be ruined.

"Tink, get me a mirror. I want to see what they look like."

I didn't know where he got it from, but he rolled over toward me, carrying a large piece of reflective glass.

Hephaistos frowned at him. "You better not have torn that off the wall."

The moment Tinker held it front of me, I gasped at how bloody cool I looked.

Each wing was a combination of brass and black metal, with brass gears affixed to two flexible points. Using my back muscles, I tried to flex them. At first, I couldn't move them much, then I pulled down and my wings expanded just that little bit further that made me look bad ass.

"Wow. This is the coolest shit I've ever seen. Heph, you are a genius, mate!"

The God didn't blush, I didn't think he had the capabilities, but he did look a bit embarrassed by the praise I was heaping on him. "Just don't kill yourself with them."

"Now, how do I fly?"

"Try squeezing with your back muscles. If that doesn't work, there is a failsafe I built in." Coming over to my side, he pointed to a switch on the strap wrapped around my middle. "Flick that and your wings will flap by themselves. But you won't have as much control on them as you would if you were moving them with your body."

Desperate to take to the sky, I flicked the switch despite Hephaistos's warnings. My wings immediately moved down, then up, and then down again, and my feet soon left the ground. I wobbled at bit as I tried to stay balanced, until I was hovering a few feet above the floor.

"This is awesome!" I shouted, grinning like a maniac.

I must've been too excited, my body moving around, because I immediately shot up toward the rocky ceiling of the forge. My wings flapped harder and faster than before.

Oh shit. I was going to crash into the ceiling or the wall.

As I soared above the forge, I saw Dionysus and Demeter pointing at me. Demeter offered a little wave as I tried to figure out how the bloody hell I was going to prevent myself from crashing into the rock and die, like a bug on a windshield. Not having any other option, I flicked off the switch.

My wings stopped flapping and I immediately started to drop to the ground.

Now, instead of being squished like a bug against the ceiling, I was going to go splat onto the stone floor. Not really the better option.

I leaned forward, kicking my legs out behind me, then squeezed my back muscles, relaxed them, then squeezed again. Tinker wheeled around on the floor below me, his arms extended, like he was going to catch me. Urgency filled me, so I closed my eyes and squeezed my back again as much as I could. If I was going to break every bone in my body, I didn't want to see it.

Then it happened. I could feel my descent slow. I opened my eyes and soared over the forge, my wings slowly flapping, keeping me airborne instead of doing a nosedive. Excited, I let out a very enthusiastic *whoop!* Dionysus and Demeter joined in, while also toasting me with their wine cups.

I did a few more swoops over the forge, trying to figure out how to land without breaking my legs and ankles. Slowly, I squeezed my back again, but didn't let it relax so I could slowly drift down to the ground. When my feet hit the floor, I relaxed and my wings drooped, though not equally, so I stumbled to the right and had to put my hand out, or else I would run into the stone staircase.

Tinker rolled over to me, happily bleeping and blooping. "You did it, Nicole. You flew like a bird!"

Sweat rolled down my back and face. Flying was hard work, especially with metal wings.

Hephaistos regarded me. It almost looked like he was impressed. "At least you didn't crash into anything. I would've been pissed if you had."

That brought a smile to my face. "Now, how do I fold my wings?"

"Press the buttons on the straps."

Glancing down, I did, and my wings retracted into the backpack-like unit strapped to my back. I felt the cords pop out of my skin, slithering back into the pack —like tiny metal snakes.

"Think I'm ready to go into battle?" I joked.

Before he could answer, Prometheus swept into the forge with a sense of urgency. "I heard from Cade. You were right. The Corpse King is after the Hours."

Hephaistos looked me right in the eyes. "Looks like you're going to get your answer soon enough."

CHAPTER TWENTY-ONE

NICOLE

$\mathcal{M}$y heart leapt in my throat. "Is Cade all right?"

"Yes, but we should go, now." Prometheus waved his hands in a circle in front of him, immediately producing a black mist.

Startled, I glanced around, I wasn't sure what I was supposed to do.

Hephaistos apparently did. He patted me on the shoulder and handed me a sword. "Good luck."

I tried to lift it, but it was really heavy. "You got a couple of daggers lying around instead?"

Taking the sword back, he replaced it with two

wicked looking knives, giving me two leg straps as sheaths too. Hephaistos fixed me up, and shoved me toward Prometheus. "Good to go."

"You are not coming?"

He shrugged. "This is what you've all been trained for. To fight the battles. I'm sitting this one out. It doesn't concern me."

"I have a feeling you're going to change your mind about that." I nodded to Prometheus. "Let's go."

He stepped into the dark shimmering fog and disappeared. I followed him in, having no clue what to expect. I didn't have to wait long or even ponder what the hell was happening, before I walked out the mist and into a gorgeous moonlit garden, blooming with lush foliage. Cade immediately stepped into view.

"Where are the others?" he asked Prometheus.

"They're on their way."

His eyes narrowed when he looked at me. "What is on your back?"

"My wings. I got them from Hephaistos. I was tired of relying on you for rides."

"I don't mind giving you rides," he defended.

Prometheus stepped up in between us. "What is the situation?"

"The guards aren't at their posts. I can't find Arcus,

who at this time of night would be here in the garden, and I saw the Pegasus fly by."

"But you haven't seen the Corpse King or any of the undead?"

He shook his head.

"Are you one hundred percent sure it was the Pegasus you saw? We had a flock of Stymphalian birds migrate up here a few hundred years ago. They are nasty, mean birds, and they can have white feathers."

"It wasn't a flock of Stymphalian birds."

He patted Cade on the shoulder, and it was a bit condescending in my opinion. By the look on Cade's face, he thought so too. "Where are the other Hours?"

"They should be in their chambers in the temple."

"Okay. Why don't the two of you check on them, while I do a perimeter check of the garden."

For a moment, Cade hesitated, but finally nodded. "Let's go, Nic."

He marched out of the garden toward the large main temple, set up on a sort of hill, and I followed him. When I caught up to Cade, I studied his profile. He was pissed off about something.

"What's wrong?"

"I don't like that Prometheus isn't taking this seriously."

"Yeah, I noticed that. The others aren't either.

When he come to get me, I was with Hephaistos, Dionysus, and Demeter. They were all drinking and had no intention of coming with me."

"I'm not surprised by that," he admitted. "None of the Gods came with us when we were sent out to prevent disasters or do a bunch of humanitarian work. I know that during the troubles last year, none of them really helped Melany, Lucian, and the others. Not directly anyway. There was some scheming behind the scenes."

"But Melany and her team were actually fighting against the Gods, weren't they?"

He nodded.

"Maybe Prometheus and the other Gods don't see any threat to themselves, so they don't really give a shit," I offered as an explanation.

"Maybe not. Although, we both know they're wrong about that."

Once inside the temple, Cade led me across the courtyard to the back side, where a whole other building seemed to reside. It was like an 18th century castle in there, with separate wings. We walked down a wide corridor with a multitude of rooms on either side.

"Do they each have their own room?" I asked.

"Yes. They spend most of their existence in their

rooms. The only time they are outside the temple walls, is when they are in the garden during their allotment."

I cringed. "That kind of sounds horrible."

"It isn't horrible or amazing. It's just what occurs. They don't think about it."

The thought of having no free will made me shudder. Of just having one singular purpose and doing it over and over again for eternity. "Maybe they do, and they just don't tell anyone." That would probably drive a thinking person completely insane.

Cade stopped at one of the closed doors and knocked. "Auge," he called through the door. "It's Cade. I'm coming in." After waiting for about three seconds, he opened the door and stepped inside the room.

Too curious to stay in the hallway, I followed him into the large, and opulently decorated palace suite that was dimly lit from sconces on the wall. Everything was cream, beige, and gold, including the floors, walls, ceiling, and every piece of furniture.

The living room had several loungers situated around the room, plumped high with silky pillows. There were endless bookshelves along the walls—I supposed to help pass the time. Although, I suspected there weren't enough books in the world to fill the eons. Also on those shelves, was a set of porcelain dolls. On the floor beneath them, I spotted a large doll house that resembled the room where we stood.

I frowned at the strangeness of it.

Before I could ask, Cade crossed the living room to a set of double doors that I assumed led to the bedroom. He knocked on those. "Auge?" He waited again for about three seconds, then opened the doors and entered.

Her room was dark, and at first, I thought it was empty, until the ruffling of bed covers echoed in the space, followed by a sleepy yawn.

"Hello?" The voice was small and quiet. Not a voice I expected from a woman.

"Auge? It's Cade. I'm very sorry to wake you."

Light slowly filled the room from the sconces on the walls, allowing me to see the large canopy bed. In it was a little girl. She appeared to be no older than nine or ten.

Her hands rubbed sleepily at her eyes, and she smiled when she spotted me behind Cade.

"Auge, this is my friend, Nicole."

"Hello, Nicole," she greeted so sweetly.

"Hey," I replied, completely taken by surprise by her appearance. I'd expected a young woman, like all the other Goddesses. I'd never seen a young Goddess or

God. Except for baby Dionysus, which was a large poke in the brain.

"Auge, have you seen Arctos? Did she come to wake you earlier than usual?" Cade asked her as she continued to yawn and rub at her eyes. Obviously, it was not time for her walk through the garden of Olympus.

She shook her head. "No, why would she do that? It is not the solstice yet."

Cade seemed to relax a little.

"Is there something wrong, Cade?"

"No, everything's fine." He gave her a sweet smile and started to back up out of the room. "We will let you go back to sleep, Auge."

I turned to leave with him but stopped in the threshold. There was something off about the space. The main door was open, when I was sure I'd closed it behind me, and there was a faint dank odor in the air. Like mothballs in an old trunk put away in the attic. There was absolutely nothing in this suite that could possibly give off that smell.

"What's wrong?" Cade asked.

Before I could answer, I saw movement out of the corner of my eye, and one of the undead leapt at me from my left. It had obviously been pressed against the wall, hiding in the shadows where I couldn't immediately see it. Hooked, crooked fingers dug into my neck as it tried to choke me, pushing me to the ground. The momentum of its attack, plus the heft of the wing pack on my back made me stumble backward, and I hit the wall.

Cade came running to my aid but was stopped by another undead, who swung a bulky metal chain toward him. The end of the chain hit Cade in the back and sent him sprawling forward. He fell onto his knees, barely missing the glass coffee table.

Frantically, I tried to pull the zombie off me, but it was digging its fingers into my skin. Pain zipped across my head and chest when its ragged nails cut me. I reached down along my right leg and withdrew the dagger strapped there. Stabbing the corpse clinging to me would do nothing, and I knew that, so I had to be clever.

Instead of plunging the blade into its nonexistence gut, I sawed at its hands until I'd cut through the bone at its wrists, and it fell off me, no longer able to hold my neck. Completely freaked out, I yanked its hands—still clinging to me—and tossed them to the floor. I was definitely going to have nightmares about that.

The undead attempted to attack me again, but without hands, it resorted to trying to bite me with jagged and broken teeth. Grabbing it by the forehead, I pushed him, keeping him back.

Concentrating on my hand, I pushed my fire power into my fingers and palms. I did it slowly, so I didn't ignite the whole room on fire like I'd done back in the barn during the first undead attack. A few seconds later, the corpse's head started to singe, the stench of its few remaining hairs burning stung my nose, then poof, its entire body disintegrated into an ash pile on the floor.

My gaze lifted from the floor, to find Cade trading blows with the other undead—Cade with a sword, the creature with that heavy metal chain. Unfortunately, the chain seemed to be inflicting more damage. Cade was favoring his right leg where it must've hit.

"Take Auge," he shouted at me. "Get her somewhere safe."

I didn't want to leave him, but I knew that the little girl was important. I rushed to the bed, where she still sat, blinking sleepily as if two corpses hadn't just broken into her room.

Pulling the blanket away from her, I grabbed her little hand. "Time to go."

"Where are we going?" she asked, but didn't put up a fight as I drew her from the bed.

"Somewhere safe for you."

"Okay," she murmured.

When I pulled her out of the bedroom, the undead fighting Cade turned toward us, swinging the chain in our direction. Clutching the girl, I threw us to the ground, feeling the metal whip swing above us. The links vibrated, rattling in the air when it passed over our heads.

Once it was gone, I picked Auge up—she was so light in my arms—and ran out of the suite, although I desperately wanted to stay and help Cade. I had to trust that he could defend himself.

I sprinted down the hallway, seeing that every previously closed door was now open, and burst out into the courtyard. I had to find Prometheus, so he could get us off Olympus and down to the academy. Auge would most definitely be safe there, behind its fortified walls and with an army to protect her. An army that I realized now, had not been called about this situation.

With the little Hour still in my arms, I ran across the courtyard and back toward the main temple. As we moved through the various chambers, I spotted a few palace guards on the ground, blood pooling around their bodies. There obviously a lot more undead in Olympus than the two who had come into Auge's suite, and they had been busy.

We were just about to cross the main exit to the

garden, when I saw movement in my peripheral vision. Someone approached me. I turned just as Iris lifted her hand and slapped me across the face. The blow whipped my head to the side, and I fumbled, struggling to keep my hold on Auge. She dropped to the ground.

"You bitch!" Iris shrieked. "How dare you show up here!" She lifted her hand to strike me again, but I wrapped my hands around her wrists to stop her.

"Iris, stop. You don't know what's actually going on right now. Olympus is under attack."

"You're a liar!" She struggled really hard in my grip, yanking and pulling, until she was able to free herself.

Before Iris could attack me again, I backed up and whipped around, looking for the little girl. "Auge?!" She wasn't in view. I couldn't see her anywhere in the chamber. "Auge?!" I shouted, terrified.

"Nicole!"

When I looked up, I found Cade running across the chamber from the courtyard. He still favored his right leg.

"What happened?" I asked him.

"It knocked me down and ran out of the suite. I couldn't catch him." His gaze swept the room, pausing a second on Iris. "Where's Auge?"

"I don't know, she fell out of my arms when I was… *interrupted*." I gestured to Iris.

Scowling, Iris's gaze bounced from Cade to me. "What the hell is going on? Did she come here with you? How dare you bring her with you?"

"Shut up, Iris," he growled. "This isn't about you."

She gasped, but something about this tone must've gotten through, because she clamped her lips tight and didn't speak further.

"She fell next to me, but must've wandered out to the garden," I urged.

Nodding, Cade and I ran outside, leaving Iris to gape some more after us.

The moment we entered the garden, two more of the undead launched at us. Cade swung his sword and cut one of them right in half. The other, that also carried a broad sword, jumped into the fray, attacking Cade. They traded blow after blow.

I started to run around, looking for Auge. At first, I didn't see her, but then the powerful whoosh of a large set of wings reverberated from the sky, and my gaze drifted upwards. The Pegasus was climbing high into the air. Twelve thick chains hung from around its body, and wrapped up in each chain was a person. An Hour.

The last one, dangling the lowest, was Auge.

Pegasus started to fade in the sky the farther it flew,

while the Corpse King kicked at its sides, encouraging the beast to fly faster. Then the sky turned white, like the blank page of a word program on a computer screen. It was the freakiest thing I'd ever seen, and that was saying something considering all that I'd been through lately.

No, I couldn't let them get away.

Heart slamming against my chest, I searched the garden, trying to figure out my options. Cade was still battling with the undead, and another one had joined the fight. I had to do something, and it was now or never.

I pushed the buttons on my pack straps and my wings shot out to the sides, connecting with my back muscles. Flicking the switch on my waist strap, I engaged them and felt them immediately start to flap, pulling me up and off the ground. I shot toward the Pegasus.

I tried to control my ascent by squeezing my back muscles, but I was more concerned with actually reaching the Pegasus, than what angle I'd be in once I did. When I'd reached the lowest chain, I tried to grab Auge, but I couldn't do it fast enough before I was propelled even higher.

Suddenly hovering at the same level as the Corpse King, I unsheathed my other dagger, intent on stabbing him with it and forcing him to guide the horse back down, but he was ready for me.

"Hello, Nicole," he growled through his twisted muzzle. "Join me in my revenge against the Gods. I know they have wronged you as well."

He offered his gnarled, gangly hand to me.

For a moment, I forgot about the twisted corpse in front of me, and remembered the man who'd been destroyed by Zeus's cruelty. I remembered seeing the dead bodies of his sons, piled high by the Gods in the city square. I remembered how sick with anger it had made me.

Then I reached out and took his hand.

Thanks for reading *Hours Of Olympus*. Don't miss all the new adventures in Demigods Academy 9! And if you loved this book, consider leaving a review on Amazon. Just one or two lines would be very helpful to support us.

Hugs,

Elisa & Kiera

ABOUT THE AUTHORS

Elisa S. Amore is the number-one bestselling author of the paranormal romance saga *Touched*.

Vanity Fair Italy called her "the undisputed queen of romantic fantasy." After the success of Touched, she produced the audio version of the saga featuring Holly-wood star Matt Lanter (*90210, Timeless, Star Wars*) and Disney actress Emma Galvin, narrator of *Twilight* and *Divergent*. Elisa is now a full-time writer of young adult fantasy. She's wild about pizza and also loves traveling, which she calls a source of constant inspiration. With her successful series about life and death, Heaven and Hell, she has built a loyal fanbase on social media that continues to grow, and has quickly become a favorite author for thousands of readers in the U.S.

Visit Elisa S. Amore's website and join her List of Readers at www.ElisaSAmore.com and Text AMORE to (844) 339 0303 for new release alerts.

FOLLOW ELISA S. AMORE:
facebook.com/eli.amore

instagram.com/eli.amore
tiktok.com/eli.amore
twitter.com/ElisaSAmore
elisa.amore@touchedsaga.com

***

Kiera Legend writes Urban Fantasy and Paranormal Romance stories that bite. She loves books, movies and Tv-Shows. Her best friends are usually vampires, witches, werewolves and angels. She never hangs out without her little dragon. She especially likes writing kick-ass heroines and strong world-buildings and is excited for all the books that are coming!

Text LEGEND to (844) 339 0303 to don't miss any of them (US only) or sign up at www.kieralegend.com to get an email alert when her next book is out.

FOLLOW KIERA LEGEND:
facebook.com/groups/kieralegend
facebook.com/kieralegend
authorkieralegend@gmail.com

Made in the USA
Middletown, DE
25 March 2023